MW00565989

Warsaw
Tales

a collection of contemporary
writing from Poland

New Europe Writers
2010

This book is dedicated to
The Travelling Reader

Contents

Acknowledgements

The editors and authors gratefully acknowledge the following:

Anne Berkeley's *The Men from Praga (first publish TLS 2001)*; Ernest Bryll *"Holiday Ode"* (first published in *Wiośnin*, Zysk i S-Ska Wydawnictwo, 2008); Jan Himilsbach's *Henke Bulbes* (from *Opowiadania Zebrane*, Wydawnictwo: Vis-à-Vis-Etudia, Krakow 2009), by kind permission the Jan Himilsbach Estate; Marek Kochan's *An Inconspicuous Man* (copyright Wydawnictwo W.A.B., 2005); Karen Kovacik's *Warsaw Architect* and *To Warsaw* (first published in *Metropolis Burning*, Cleveland State University Poetry Centre 2005); *At the Church of St James in Ochota, Warsaw*, (first published in *Crab Orchard Review vol. 6 no. 2)*; *My Polish Widower* (first published in the *Robert Owen Butler Fiction Prize Anthology*, 2004); Jacek Podsiadło's *Millennium Drift (The Life, and Specifically the Death of Angelica de Sancé*, Wydawnictwo Znak, Kraków, 2008); Stephen Romer's *Sailing to Sopot (Plato's Ladder*, OUP,1993); Carole Satyamurti's *Feast of Corpus Christi* (first published in *Sixty Women Poets*, Bloodaxe Books, 1994); Sławomir Shuty's *Evolution* (copyright Wydawnictwo W.A.B., 2005); Lisa Siedlarz's *"Wigilia"* (first published in the 2007 Anthology of Kritya, Chettkunnyu, India); John Surowiecki's *"Chopin Mazurka in A Minor"* (first published in The Innisfree Poetry Journal 5, Sept. 2007); Joanna Szczepkowska's *Mid Air* (first published as *„W powietrzu"* from *„Ludzie ulicy i inne owoce miłości"* Wydawca: Nowy Świat, 2006); Leo Yankevich's *The Idiot* (first published in *The Windsor Review)* and *"Eastertide"* (first published in *Chronicles).*

Any errors or omissions will be corrected in subsequent editions.

Editorial Note

The history of writers is marked by a habit of banding together individuals into groups, not least by time and place.

New Europe Writers began in a café on Nowogrodzka where a semi-Canadian Polish journalist, with a connection to Radio Free Europe, ran a café as a cover for his catering business.

Open to the needs of the scribbler, Stash owned the only bar not to close when the G-whiz summit boarded-out the centre of town ahead of the global protesters. *'Come and have a drink after the riot'* was painted across the plate glass.

There were no riots. But a poet, a playwright and a writer went and had a drink anyway. And what emerged was a creative partnership which continues to grow.

Writing is solitary. But all work sits within a context. Around half of the contributors to this volume are, in this context, NEW writers. They can be identified because their work has already appeared in one or more of NEW's previous collections - the successful 'Prague Tales' and 'Budapest Tales'.

As with the earlier volumes, the familiar names are leavened with an admixture of established and unfamiliar names, to ensure that the picture painted in these pages is of the real Poland - one that can be recognised by those who live there and those who travel through.

This is the third volume in a ten year project to capture the spirit of New Europe. Centred on a city, each collection seeks to leave the armchair traveller with a unique sense of place. And give the visitor a glimpse into the country that is hidden from the casual tourist: the humorous, the satiric, and the ironic Poland, quite as much as the country whose future lies in the past.

Keep your curtains open: you may be surprised what's out there to see.

The Editors
New Europe Writers

This Notion of Warszawa - Ewa Kowalczyk

Would you think it so indecent of me if one day,
noticing your car on Ujazdowskie's grand Aleji-
I - just like that- got in, sat next to you, as lonely
strangers do on benches in Łazienki park, but only
you would have the gear lever next to you as well
and armrests shaped in perfect circle, in the swell
of traffic on Róż Junction; at that turn you take
I'd hope you, smiling, would in providence mistake
the lever for my knee, though I'll confess I don't
know what would then ensue, when drivers, wont
to stop at green lights, keep us waiting in a queue.
Pursue the notion no one's there, but me and you?

So licentious if I had you drive me to Old Town,
had Sigismund, atop his column, then look down
in envy of us two together in his castle-keep arena,
come to admire our Mermaid Statue, bold Syrena
brandishing her sword above the terra-cotta roofs
of vintner's houses, as a droshky's horse's hooves
clack on the cobbled streets. Or would you rather
I resigned from this romantic notion of Warszawa
and had you take me back to Ujazdowskie where
I stood waiting for that tram of empty seats and air
of feeling such an act would have been so long ago.
Would you believe all this about us both were so?

Translated by Stefan Bodlewski

Plan Miasta Warszawy - Karen Kovacik

Your Kino Moscow gleams like a pink dish
with the films of Clint Eastwood and French farce.
I feel like an umbrella in for repair.
I'd rather be a telescope, to see past
the scrim of things American,
to smell past pickles, smoke, and grief
and understand the idiom of uprisings.

You are the map that exists and the ones that have disappeared.
You are the cigarette that makes the slow bus come.
I'm a thin glass of oolong, lucky in lust,
in this province of lip and teeth
where syllables squeak like sugar
and our hands are always hot
and my marriage dies on double beds of cake.

You are a museum of ailing clocks,
you are streets named Barley, Gold, and Starch.
I watch a man on a train eat a tomato
like an apple. He keeps checking his pockets
for spies. Why so nervous? I wonder.
He licks his fingers and whispers:
"The Jews, they're everywhere."

You are the church and the candles in the church,
the bank and the money, the book and the words.
I avoid talk. My bangs are trimmed
by the centimeter. The hives look like dollhouses
and Józek feeds me raw honey.
Although I'm afraid, I watch and taste.

The New World - Hatif Janabi

On New World Street, in its usual labour pains, where vigilant lenses observe naked truths, where the cameras of the day have no time for reflection, I saw door handles shaped like lions and shut doors staring from the balcony of the old world. I touched them with the lightness of a shy expert, and when I stared at the hidden reliefs, I found, carved in bronze, the names of lovers who died defending the city and, in another corner, names of authors and artists who passed away long ago.

On New World Street I sipped coffee and watched two lovers whisper to each other, and from the end of a hall crowded with expressionist paintings, a famous local song blared.

Central Station - Jacek Dehnel

What drove them to come here, among the tables
of the station's chrome and coarse design
with its foreign lexis ("latte", "donat", "mocha")
and apparent comfort? What important holiday-
granddaughter's first communion, godson's wedding?-
drew them from their apartment by bob and cap,
tossed them from one ticket-office to the next
and had their green valise full of ordinary things
rumble across the Central Station's slabs?
                    He, with an elegance
a trifle lower class, she in her "facial shoes",
he carrying her golden-patterned cream handbag,
she telling him: "Staś, you'd prefer …"- a loud shout interrupts –
"- … wouldn't you? Take this chocolate, then". What culture
did create her antediluvian hairdo, his neckerchief, her
unfashionable jacket. They're like a pair of tritons
that some capricious current has washed up on the coast
of cast-out material, an heraldic relief you find, surprised,
between the logos of Reserved and Empik.

Translated by Wojciech Maślarz

Heńka Bulbes and Co - Jan Himilsbach

Our district had been a total shambles since time immemorial. No big surprise to the residents, however, who took this for granted. But it all came to a head the day the neighborhood cop, nicknamed Mussolini, told his boss he'd had enough and took some leave.

Mussolini knew the folk on his patch like the back of his hand, who was with whom, when and why. Staff Sergeant Tufta, on the other hand, was his temporary replacement and as green as a plank. Shy, distant, aware he was not in for a long haul, Tufta wasn't interested in anyone, or improving anything. He'd occasionally put in an appearance. But nothing more.

To make maters worse, the seasons also made their contribution. Along came May, not often as fine as this, and the thoughts of all, regardless of age, turned to sex. Not least the youths from the local high school.

Lads with down beginning to appear on their upper lips, unable to escort a decent girl across the street in style, would once or twice accost Heńka Bulbes in the company of her friend, Sroka the Magpie, who both operated down-town for their earnings.

The two girls waltzed into the street straight out of the hair dresser where the owner was known as a playboy. Heńka with her hair done up in chestnut, Sroka the Magpie for a change opting for blonde. From a distance they reeked of Eau-de-Cologne, but on closer inspection you could see the salon's owner had got off to a good start and made a jolly zlot that morning.

Positioning themselves on opposite sides of the street, they attempted to stop some 'wheels' But no wheels would stop. As for repairing to Café Coquette - in this heat - it would be madness. Furious, they were at the end of their tether when some recent school leavers arrived on the scene, four of them.

"Hey, where are you off to, girls?" the overgrown youngest of them propositioned Heńka. Staring back at the boy, she noted the rising desire burning in his eyes. Behind him stood his friends of the same age, kitted out in cotton T-shirts with Adidas signs and jeans bleached by sun and rain

"What do you say, girls? Let's go?" a boy asked, then turning to Heńka. "You're two, as I can see, we're four. A perfect sextet, sweet-hearts. One for two. And two for one. Us." he proffered pointing to his mates, "Club together; each two tens and in six we'll put on a bash, have some big fun."

"For two tens, little boy, you can buy an ice-cream," she firmly retorted and pointed to the nearby cake shop in front of which a large queue had formed.

"But we want to have some fun."
"So go home to your mummy and have fun there for two tens." Heńka suggested.
"What did you say?" the boy was surprised. "Repeat that."
"You heard me."

The lad wanted to jump at Heńka with his nails, but she stopped him and then the unexpected: a so far peaceful, even friendly and smiling Heńka Bulbes suddenly shouted straight into the lad's face:

"Go to back to the blackboard jungle, you little brat! Swat up for tomorrow's written Polish exam."

The lad sprung back from the girl, as if from a punch. While Heńka was occupied with a heated exchange with the boy, Sroka flagged down a taxi and the two girls got in.

"What did they want from you?" Sroka asked.
"Nothing of the sort. Not what you're thinking."
"Where to, ladies?" the driver asked, peeking at them through the rear-vision mirror.
"Turn left into the junior high school," said Heńka.
"What are you up to?" Sroka was anxious. "What in blazers.. we're supposed to go to ... Café Coquette'?"
"I need to enroll you in a school," said Heńka cheerfully. And to the driver, "Continue."

They moved on, after five minutes pulled up in front of the main entrance to the junior high school.

"Please wait. We'll be back and then we'll be go into the city."

The two girls marched into the headmaster's office.

"What brings you here, Henia?" the headmaster said with delighted surprise, stepping out from behind his desk to welcome Heńka Bulbes.

"Sir," Heńka came to the point. "Without wasting your precious time, I will tell you at once what concerns me. Before I embarked on this road to vice, you'd been teaching me for many a year. Times may have changed, but as an alumni of these hallowed walls, I will not abide you having your students accost decent women in the street in broad daylight. My friend and I were on our way to work, when your students in a boorish manner.. oh, there they go, the four of them..."

"But it doesn't surprise me in the least that such gorgeous ladies as yourselves..." said the headmaster cheerfully. "Indeed, I rather regret myself I'm not their age and that I am holding such an exposed managerial position."

In the taxi Sroka-The-Magpie could not restrain herself:

"And what was that all about? Everyone in the city knows that you, Heńka Bulbes, are an trollop from way back, but not till now did I know you was a first-class rat."

Lost in thought, Henka could only respond with:

"I care about the 'good' name of the school."

And so they promptly proceeded to Café Coquette which was frequented by Arabs.

Translated by Katarzyna Waldegrave

Holiday Ode - Ernest Bryll

Happy are they, who together with us
Push trolleys in the supermarts
And proudly stand at checkout counters
Like The Elect at Heaven's Gate.

Happy are they, who with their families
Gobble Big Macs at MacDonald's,
Munching on such buns, they'll not
Taste all tender flavours of the universe.

Recollection of another world does not
Suppress their souls. They have all
They ever wanted at a price affordable

And though they watch nightmares only
On TV, they sleep as if enchanted
Quietly, shallowly and memory-free.

Translated by Karolina Maślarz and John a'Beckett

The Man Upstairs - James G. Coon

The man living upstairs from me has been renovating his apartment for nine years, maybe longer, they tell me. No one knows for sure. The previous occupant of my apartment died (old age, they say). I have been living here for the past two years and can personally vouch for renovation activity during that period of time. Every so often, Pan Dupek, as I have christened him, gives in to a perverse craving for loud banging noises. This can happen at any time of the day or night.

One nail at a time, by God.

Home was not rebuilt in a day!

Bang! Bang! Bang!

Then his dementia goes into remission, and the banging stops.

His wife slipper-shuffles for a while and the dog goes tippitty-tappitty for a couple of laps around Chez Dupek, then it is quiet again. This is the normal routine, but from time to time he tries for a new personal best. On the most spectacular such occasion he spent two days trying to pound a hole through his kitchen floor with a sledgehammer. At least that's what it sounded and felt like. The whole building shook. "New Zealand here we come!" I thought.

BOOM! BOOM! BOOM!

His kitchen is directly over mine, so it was only a matter of time. No point in warning the guy. His kind always knows better.

I arrived home from work to find a trail of plaster chunks and dust in the hall leading to a much larger accumulation on my kitchen floor and surrounding surfaces. Dust to dust, eh? Someone is either coming or going around here, and it ain't me, I thought. In fact, nearly half of my thick plaster kitchen ceiling was in capitulatory repose on my kitchen floor, having surrendered in the struggle to find peace on this earth. I stomped up the stairs to beard the dupek in his den.

"Well, you finally succeeded. My ceiling is now on the floor," I told him.

"Yeah, yeah, right," he said. "OK, come and look," I said.

He swaggered down the stairs sporting one of those omniscient commie smirks you see chiseled into every cement-head in Central Europe. He saw the mess, grabbed his head with both hands, grimaced wildly, reeled backward on his heels like some cartoon character, and cried out: KURCZE!

Truer words are rarely spoken, I thought.

"Now do you believe me?" I asked. "And while you're at it, who is going to clean up this mess?"

"KURCZE!" he cried out again. "I'll fix the ceiling, don't worry, I'll fix the ceiling."

"Forget the ceiling! Who is going to clean up this mess?" I asked.

He wobbled back upstairs like a chimpanzee with diarrhea, still holding his head with both hands, muttering "kurczę kurczę." Shortly thereafter, his wife plodded down the stairs, shaking and sweating, and made a half-hearted attempt to sweep up. Forget it before you have a heart attack, I told her. Well, she is rather old, though not exactly frail. Pani Krowa, if you know what I mean. It was now about 7PM. I called the landlady's sister (the landlady does not live nearby).

"Half the kitchen ceiling fell on the floor and it's a big mess," I told her. "Well, can it wait until tomorrow?" she asked. "Yeah, but it really is a very big mess," I said. A couple of minutes later she called back:

"My husband and I are coming over to look at it," she said. "OK," I said, "but looking at it won't clean it up, and it is a very big mess." "We want to see just how big of a mess it is," she said. "OK," I said. "I'll be here."

They arrived. The husband looked, reeled back on his heals and cried out KURCZE! Then the wife peaked around the corner into the kitchen, reeled back on her heals and cried out KURCZE!

"Now do you believe me?" I asked. "I told you nearly half of the ceiling was on the floor and there it is, right?" "Yeah," they agreed despondently. They seemed genuinely disappointed about missing an opportunity to make fun of 'a typical exaggerating American.' "Well, what now?" I asked. "OK, we'll clean it up," they said. So we all pitched in and pitched out the debris, more or less. The next day the local "pani cleaningowa" finished the job, adding her own belated "KURCZE" to the chorus.

The ceiling still needed to be repaired, but of course, first and foremost, the cooperative association had to determine blame.

As it happens, the man upstairs is Prezes of the cooperative. You can probably see where this is leading.

So Pan Prezes assembled a delegation of the usual mouth-breathing sycophants to inspect the premises and render a fair and impartial opinion. They arrived along with the landlady's sister. The delegation consisted of one old lady who works for Pan Prezes in the office and some old guy carrying a yard stick who spent the whole time staring open-mouthed at the ceiling mumbling incomprehensibly. Pan Prezes was in his full glory, hands in pockets, rocking fore and aft, heel-to-toe-to-heel, grinning the biggest shit-eating grin I have ever seen on what is purported to be a human being. After 25 minutes of wandering about aimlessly, staring skyward, and babbling back and forth, Pan Prezes declared the inspection complete and stated that the delegation would render a final opinion in writing in one week.

'Gee,' I thought, 'this is going to be a real cliff-hanger. I can hardly wait to find out what they decide.'

The fateful day arrived, and as I suspected, the jury returned a verdict of not guilty regarding Pan Prezes and pinned the rap on the building. The written statement actually said: "the building is guilty." Consequently, my landlady had to pay for the repairs. Not Pan Prezes, not the cooperative, and not even the building. Fortunately, not me either. I had been waiting to see if they could think of a way to hang it on me. Perhaps something like: "excessive localized gravity due to the presence of an overly serious alien force." Understandably, the building itself was unavailable for further comment, having already expressed its opinion of Pan Prezes by dropping its load on my kitchen floor in the first place. Incredibly, the landlady's sister actually thought there had been a chance that the delegation would declare Pan Prezes guilty. I had no idea anyone over the age of six months was that naïve, and she is WELL over the age of six months.

I went away over Christmas and when I came back it was all fixed. All things considered, it was a relatively painless resolution to an idiotic situation, except that some of the people in my office agreed that the building was guilty! They said it was old, probably not very well constructed in the first place (like so many other things, including their stupid argument), and no repairs had been done in a long time by my landlady.

I told them none of that was true and that if they had been there and felt the building shaking on its foundation while Pan Prezes sledge-hammered his way to infamy, they would probably think differently.

They just shook their heads and went back to work.

I'm sure they were thinking: "just another typical exaggerating American."

KURCZE!

Chopin Mazurka in A Minor - John Surowiecki

It passes the childhoods of people
it doesn't know, meeting aunts
with hennish stop-and-go eyes
and uncles with tiny square teeth.

It consoles the suddenly parentless,
has lunch with exiting lovers,
wanders through the park
holding hands with someone who
relies on it more than it likes.

Sensing it is gradually being replaced
by memory and remorse.
A high-school girl takes up its theme,
then goes on to something else.

The Sworn Translator - John a'Beckett

A Warsaw dream above the city's Soviet reality
ten storeys high, Pan Kuszmek, old survivor
so humble at his oaken desk, translator sworn
to lean upon my tattered Melbourne Arts degree
inspecting it for watermark, age, origin, validity
"Now this ...reminds me of my oath. I had to swear.."
his English cutting through accented thickness, clear
"that every word.."- he says in sun-lit and Slavonic air -
"...translated must be quite exact. A dream, that oath.
For though two languages may share a common tree,
This Polish had, I do confess, a very different growth"

Sun happens into winter, and a waving heat
beats warm on pipes, as if a tired drummer has
us both imagining an endless summer as

my eyes fall on the odd shapes on his wall:
strange paper-mache maps of things: Pantopia
all put together with a sworn translator's hands,
a saddle for a horse with wings, Symphonic Street's
receding menu from the Happenstance Hotel,
a non-existent Moscow, or a Warsaw meant-to-be.
"Too old to travel, I make journeys of the mind...
what's left of my imagination is a good, I find,
companion and an even better guide. I've been
to places other people have looked forward to:
wheres, whens they rather hoped they'd seen"

I nod agreement as I also find these icons do
share with old Soviet reality a sense of déjà vu.

Warsaw Architect - Karen Kovacik

Let there be modernism, he says, and in the radiant flat world
arising on his square of bristol, a cube shimmers.
Then balconies appear, and freshly waxed floors, and kitchens
still innocent of grease and smoke. Will he add
some tall cones of cedar or a brush tip of poplar?
Anything is possible beneath the thin gouache sky.

His own apartment is a wreck of central planning:
low ceilings, cracked tile, the orange linoleum
of some Seventies' utopia. Exposed wires
dangle in the hall, the lift reeks of garbage.
A Freudian billboard obscures the house number
with praise for a cigarette "both strong and hard."

How does he move between these realms?
What passport of intellect or spirit allows him
to forsake parabola and grid for this corridor
weeping with onions? On his screen,
Warsaw appears flat as paper, a page erased by fire,
before granite dreams of coalminers holding up the world.

Outside a cold rain, chimneys and pavement
the colour of tea, women hauling in stockings
from the balconies. I love the hand's provisional flourish,
before the first line, when anything can emerge –
even this Austrian market with suburban shoppers,
even this highrise of breakfast flakes, this Danube of soda.

Co mają tak za tak... - Andrew Fincham

I opened my eyes.

Like the woman in Mickiewicz's 'Good Morning,' there were flies around my mouth, and it was not obvious if I were living or dead.

I dimly recalled some words of a late poetess: Death leaves Us homesick. Experience proving best to distrust pronouncements in poems which play with punctuation, especially near dawn, I pulled the pillow over my head.

And besides, I was sick of home.

*

The world is divided (according to some) into those who hate to travel and those who purport to love it. To the first, it's not clear where lies the thrill of waking up in a strange bed. For the second, some pursue an almost atavistic worship of the multi-labelled cabin trunk, carried by capped bell boys in hand-cranked lifts. The rest discover merit in going unwashed whilst being eaten by mosquitoes on a Bangkok beach for a fiver.

Both sorts, it seems to me, are probably unhappy.

So my path into Warsaw (as subsequently recorded between my father's place of birth and mother's maiden name on a policeman's notebook in a hotel foyer) was unlooked for. It came about as a result of a telex that arrived on the mat of a London flat but which appeared to originate from beyond the grave:

HURRY – NEED ARRANGE FUNERAL - DINT

Not for the first time, I found I was bequeathed a slight feeling of guilt to fill the place of an aged relative. Perhaps I could have made more of an effort to keep in touch. The loneliness of a name on an annual Christmas card is suddenly weighed in the balance. Perhaps unconsciously, the thought of the departed's signature produces a subliminal reminder of testatory dispositions and the length of a visit shrinks before the sudden proximity of an inheritance.

So it was with my Great Uncle Dintenfass.
Born in the mists of time outside Tarnów, Uncle Dint had by his death become a living legend. Half believed and often out of this world, his tales of Galician

24

life reached back almost a century, and never failed to feature the great departed in whose subsequent successes my relative had taken a hand. One of the more elaborate storytellers of his age, it would seem that his age had finally told against him, and I counted the loss heavier than I had expected.

A certain closeness over the years had kept us from drifting apart, although we'd always lived at opposite ends of the continent. But since we'd neither spoken nor corresponded (seasonal greets excepted) in years, I was rather surprised to be summoned to serve in an executory capacity. The old boy must have remembered me after all.

And I consoled myself with that thought.

*

Several telexes and a Lot flight later I was a hot potato in a passionate game of exchange which took place about the revolving doors of the Hotel Sovietski. The main characters were an irate taxi driver, waving a sheaf of several million zloty (formerly in my possession) and the receptionist, a most attractive girl whose vocabulary I understood to be surprisingly extensive from the browbeaten appearance it was imparting to her adversary. A walk-on part by a policeman, originally invoked by the cabbie, provided a neat twist when he took the side of the angel, and relieving the ugly of the better part of his fare, restored both me and my baggage to the bed-side of the doors.

'Not a good man' shrugged the beauty with a warning shake of the head, as if I were a child caught talking to a stranger. The officer of the law now proffered her the remains of my fare, of which she took the larger share and handed it to me with a satisfied smile which apparently closed the matter.

Ever since I'd trod the warm asphalt of Okęcie, I'd wondered why I was behind the wall. Of course, the wall was down, as evinced by the ease with which I'd acquired my visitor's *wisa*. But it had not been for long, and the tenements astride the widely-broken streets still had a coldish look to them, under a broad summer sun. I wondered how much had changed, and found I'd done so aloud.

'Barbeque' she said, her exquisite face momentarily withdrawn from the register. Surprised, I asked if that was due to better weather. Or the availability of meat.

'Now there is barbeque. To buy in Galleria. Before, we have fire in summer, outside.'

She handed over a key. 'Enjoy Warsaw Sobieski Hotel.'

'Sobieski? You don't pronounce it Sovietski, then?' I began to suspect the cause of my circumspectious taxi tour.

'Jan III Sobieski: King of Poland, Grand Duke Lithuania, Ruthenia, Prussia, Masovia, Samogitia, Livonia, Smolensk, Kiev, Volhynia, Podlasie, Severia, and Chernihiv. And maybe some other places.'

'A rose by any other name...' I proffered, in some confusion.

'Szekspira. Romeo i Julia.'

I thanked her, bowed, and retreated.

*

The next morning I arrived early at the Filtrowa address of my late relative by the simple measure of securing the services of the hotel cab, and paced the quiet pavements in pensive mood awaiting the appointed time. Despite a succession of terse communications, I remained at a slight loss as to what, exactly, I was there to do.

But the sight of the elegant villa opened my eyes to a new world, one which ran less upon the loss of my Slavic relict than on personal gain, net of funerary expenses. I pictured a future where I would be educated and entertained in equal measure by the engagingly endowed Sobieski Juliet, a dream only broken when a dapper old fellow appeared from behind the high gate holding an iced tumbler in one grey-gloved hand and a small flask in the other.

'When you find you've had as much as you want of the pavement,' instructed my Uncle Dint with the slightest wink towards the bottle, 'do come in and make yourself at home.'

*

It wasn't until two mornings later that I came to and had the chance to explain why my relative's appearance had caused me to faint. In falling, I'd struck my head upon some remnant of cast iron street-furniture in which that quarter is still rich, and the 'Returned to Life' party that Uncle threw in order to celebrate my discharge from hospital almost sent me back.

I was lying in bed, oblivious of the good morrow, when a tap on the door preceded his arrival bearing what appeared to be a medicinal preparation glowing greenly through a dim glass. He wrapped it in my shaking fingers.
'Doctor's orders!'
I drank it with a weak smile.
The pain arrived at my head, lungs and heart at the same time. I could speak but one word, and that weakly.
'Water!'
The relative was reassuring.
'Never water a 'Prairie Fire'! Enough to turn St. Bruno a bishop!' He saw an opening for digression, and slipped through. 'But true *Chartreuse* illicits *Illicium verum*[1]. Perhaps it's the tabasco, then, that's ticklish...'
'I'm on fire!'
'You're perhaps thinking of a flaming Sambuca?'
'Coffee!' It appeared to be my only hope.
'*Sambuca con mosca?* With flies? Who gives a bean for health, hope and happiness, as they say...'
He drew back the curtain and flooded the room with Warsaw summer sun.
'Take care when mixing up your drinks my boy....'
'I'm dying...'
He shook his head, gently.
'No. I am.'

*

We met again at a rather delayed breakfast.
As I violated the crisp linen, my host entered the room and stood before the sideboard.
I spoke first.
'I'm sorry I'm late.'
'Not that I'm not?'
I rephrased.
'I regret my delayed arrival.'
'Not my early departure?'
'I'm sorry I'm late.'
'I'm not.'
'I know...'
'I'm rather glad I'm not.'
'I, too...'

---

[1] Star Anise

27

There was an almost imperceptible pause.

'Coffee?'
I accepted with a nod.
The toast crunched.

I was wondering how to approach the object of my visit with its subject when my relative jumped in with both feet.
'I'm not unwell. I want you to know that. In fact, I've never felt fitter. I could give the legendary Galahad a run for his money.'
'Sir Galahad: the perfect knight?'
'The Honourable[2]. But yes, on a good night. On the flat, of course. Never over the sticks.'

I let it drop. 'So why the urgent summons for the funeral?'

Uncle Dint put down his cup with care.

'You speak from the valley of youth. We on the summits of life see further. Perhaps our sleeping Knight, the massif Gievont, may see furthest of all. But of course, being asleep, rather than dead, the issue of a final resting place does not apply in his case.'

I waved aside the impermanence of the Tatras and indicated he should move on.

'Let me paint you a picture.'

*

'Our Polish nation's history,' began my Uncle Dint, 'is something of a curate's egg. And whilst we're proud to celebrate the parts of it which have been excellent, it is only just to admit the claim that the bad has provided us with quite as much off which to live. At least for those whose roots to our soil have been replanted abroad. In that respect, we may be considered slightly Irish, but you never heard me say that.

---

[2] A search through the Dintenfass Archive suggests the Hon. G.Threepwood [Ed]

'Our history then, is part of our present, and because of this, part of our future, too. If we're not very careful, we'll be living our past until the end of time. But let that pass.

'The slicing and dicing of politics by generals has minced us finer than a *foie gras*. I'm no champion of the ducks, unless I'm dining at Kamienne Schodki. – in fact I'd always prefer to hang a brace for a week or so - I find them more to my taste. *Chacun à son gout.* But perhaps no *gavage* has been more unpalatable than the diet on which we were force-fed after the last war. We were hungry, certainly. But perhaps it had been better to starve. But I digress.'

It was with a sense of foreboding that I noted, for the very first time, that my relative returned to the topic in hand before the season due. He sighed and began afresh.

'Do you remember a painter named Stanisław?' I shook my head. 'Stanisław Witkiewicz, the one who nearly went to America…'
'I never knew that. I thought he killed himself.'
'No, that was another painter named Stanisław Witkiewicz. I'm talking about his father.'
'Then no.'
'He nearly went to America. But he didn't. He stayed. Because he could not bring himself to leave.'
It sounded reasonable.
'But when your home has been lost, where can you hope to stay?'
I sympathised. Great Uncle Dint was, after all, a Galician.
'His son, of course, I knew in Warsaw.'
I feigned surprised.
'I advised him to travel after Jadwiga left us. But his glass was ever half empty.' The words appeared to remind my Uncle of something, for he turned his back momentarily to reappear with his cup refreshed.

'He fell to pieces when Stalin's piglets came. So they buried him - for a while. Then they dug him up.' He looked at me with an intensity I'd seldom seen. '…Yes, they dug him up. Someone apparently wanted to move him to Zakopane. Well, why not, you may feel?' I shrugged.
'They dug him up and shipped him down from the back end of beyond. Because they thought he should be buried at home.'
He drained the cup. There was more to come.
'Not too long ago, some fellows took a look at what was left inside the

coffin. And found his were the remains of some Ukrainian woman.'
The cup rattled in the saucer.

'That's not going to happen to me.'

Breakfast was over.

*

Sometime later we were strolling along the thoroughfare which links Warsaw's New Town to the Old, and it was perhaps a succession of signs offering *kaczka pieczona z jablkami* that got my Great-Uncle back in the hunt.

'An apple a day keeps the Doctor away!' he opined, as we gained the square. I refrained from comment. 'But duck can bring a surprise... It's all in the name.'

From his youth, he said, he had been alert to the potential of names and indeed, used many in his early experiences as a boarder dossing amongst the lesser inhabitants of the *haut monde*. His predilection for the *nom de plume* extended to his collection of passports, of which he kept a selection issued by several authorities and which ascribed to him a selection of both nationalities and names.

'Horses for Courses' he would say, as we approached a border. And it must be admitted that I never once saw him flourish documentation without being whisked off to what he would later describe as the VIP suite under some kind of guard of honour, more often than not armed.

In the manner of names, Uncle divulged (as we took coffee in a café under the fixed gaze of an iron basilisk while watching children splash in the Siren's gutter), that he had once fallen heavily under the influence of a clear-sprung philologist from Białystok, part of whose *Lingwe uniwersala* he'd found on a park bench in Veisiejai when stalking duck. He'd spotted what appeared to be a party of three shoveler[3], when his attention was drawn to a striking fellow with a most luxuriant beard but not a trace of hair on his head.

---

[3] The Northern Shoveler *Anas clypeata* rather than the Red cousin *Anas platalea*, obviously. From this it can be safely assumed the event took place in summer.

Suspecting a disguise, and sensing a fellow *anasophile*, my relative approached the beaver in a roundabout manner[4] and introduced himself as Thomas Thorsteinsson, then his favoured alias when inside the Russian Empire. The fellow replied in kind, indicating that he went under the name of Lyudovik, named Eliezer (although the certificate used the Yiddish form Leyzer).

Uncle Dint was on the point of constructing a pleasantry concerning the practice of Christian names, when the beard continued.

'However, I have only today decided to be known as Lazar, putting aside forever the gentile connection. If I tell you I have also decided to renounce the patronymic Markovich, you will no doubt recognise that I have undergone a most thorough revision of conventions of conversational address.'
'Call me Tom,' opened Uncle Dint, offering his hand.
'Call me Ludo,' said the Beaver.

Their subsequent lunch was memorable. Whilst introducing his new friend to the *Provençal pistou*, Uncle explaining that the sauce was essentially pesto without the seeds of the *pinus*, he found his companion's attention compelled towards clarifying their mode of communication rather than clearing his plate.

'I explained to him it was merely a simplified set of common ingredients, mixed up. He kept repeating, as we were eating, 'near pesto.' He wrote it down several times. It was only as the meal drew to a close I found he'd anagramatised it.

And that's how Uncle Dint got Dr. L.L Zamenhof started in the Esperanto business.

*

The talk of lunch moved us swiftly across the market square to top of the stone steps and a table at the Uncle's favoured source of roasted duck with apple.

'Of course, he really changed his name to avoid confusion with his brother, the sawbones Dr. L. Zamenhof,' he said as the waiter uncorked a most reasonable rose and retired.

---

[4] The recreational equipment currently visible in the park was installed at a much later date. [Ed note]

'I don't quite see...'

'You're not a philologist – the second L makes all the difference in the world. Think of the Welsh.'

'This square' he expanded, 'always serves to remind me it's about time to return to Krakow.' He gave small sigh. 'Perhaps I should be buried there?'

'Amongst the kings?'

'Some of them. Of course, there's no house of Mickiewicz there – I can highly recommend the beer in the cellar as an essential part of any Warsaw visit. But do mind the steps. But on the whole, there's a spirituality about that city which we somehow failed to carry here when we took over the capital. Or it was lost it in the intervening four hundred years.'

'Perhaps it will come back?'

'Time will tell.'

He looked thoughtful.

'Zamenhof, of course, remained a true Pole.'

'How does one tell that?'

'Language. I remember he wrote to me a little after that first lunch. If I recall correctly he said '*Mia gepatra lingvo estas la rusa; sed nun mi parolas pli pole...*[5] Or words to that effect.'

I sipped the wine in silence.

'Cat got your tongue?' Uncle Dint was playful. 'Or is it more a case of Wittgenstein's seventh proposition?'[6]

I nodded incomprehension.

'Of course, we can still count on the old place to turn out capital chaps when we need them.'

I asked him who he was talking about, wishing at the same time I might clarify 'what.'

'Young Karol Wojtyła.'

I remained blank.

'Christian Karol – the keenest keeper in Wadowice! I helped him chose his first pair of boots. They're going to make him a saint, you know. *Santo Subito*! And rightly so.'

'You're not referring to the Pope?'

'Quite right my boy. No-one here has stopped calling him that. Jan Paweł II will always be the Father for us.'

---

[5] Letter to Th. Thorsteinsson dated 8th March 1901

[6] '*Wovon man nicht sprechen kann, darüber muß man schweigen.*' Tractatus Logico-Philosophicus 1921

'You knew him?' I was incredulous.

'Of course. He was a Galician. We were practically neighbours.' Great Uncle Dint beamed, as he always did at a mention of his homeland.

'What's that about boots?'

'I remember most clearly. He was outside a cobbler's on Wąska, admiring the wide selection of natty footwear. I advised him most strongly: it's not the upper you need to think about. It's the strength of the sole.'

I coughed slightly.

'And the importance of dubbin. I like to think he remembered that.'

And that's how Uncle Dint got Karol Wojtyła out of the goal-saving business.

*

The sun was still high in the sky as we strolled back home, the fumes of the traffic from the old busses as we left the New World and headed along Jerozolimskie.

'Jerusalem's no good for Pope's, now, of course.' Uncle mused as we came in sight of the Palace of Culture.' Of course, they buried him in the Vatican. At least they popped on the shelf where the Blessed John XXIII used to be. And that was because they'd made a space by moving him indoors. So you see, there is no knowing when they'll try and move him on. Bring him home. Or a part of him. It must be a worry.'

We stepped aside the main road to skirt towards Uncle's home, along Nowogrodzka, with the sound of various instruments floating from open windows in the sudden quiet of the evening.

'You look like you're in need of a rest,' my relative informed me as we drew alongside a bustling café. Parking me on a small table outside, he disappeared inside, returning quite some time later with two large glasses of beer. 'I had to have a word with Stash,' he said, as if by way of explanation. 'First class fellow – knows everybody worth knowing. Never forgets.' He took a draught of beer. 'But he can go on, rather.'

We sat drinking in the evening. I felt I was beginning to understand why I was there.

'You think we need some sort of Sepulchre?'

Uncle Dint looked grave. He produced a long cigar, and cut it with deliberation.

'Walled in?' He lit a match, and began to rotate the tip, cultivating the flame
'You'd feel imprisoned?' I was not entirely surprised.
'Use your head. Stone walls do not a prison make. Poe faced his fears.
Although I believe he had a bell installed.'
'Do you have any strong feelings about the afterlife?' I felt I should ask.
'There's no smoke without fire.' He shook the match and his head. "Cervantes:
a genuine Montecristo – one can count on that...' He appeared to be
approaching contentment. 'I remember the smoke from the torches in the
Rynek at Kraków the night they brought Our Lady of Fátima round on a
tray. I was dining with a young woman in a curtained booth at Wierzynek,
on tinned peas and a steak which appeared to have been acquired in 1364,
while beyond the windowpane, amidst the snow, thousands paraded in
hat's and scarves and glory in their hearts. We descended to take a better
look, and stepped into a cloud of love. I was most disconcerting. But it was
most definitely the case.'

He looked almost serious for a moment, and tapped the end of the cigar.
'Ashes to ashes.'

He motioned to the bar tender, who returned almost immediately with brim-
ming glass which sparkled in the late sun. 'It's the fate of poets, I suppose, to
die unread. From Ned Beg to poor old Edward King, he of the watery bier.'
He took a long sip.

I noted that my Uncle seemed fixated with death. But there seemed no good
reason.

'You seem bitter?'
'That's putting it mildly.'
'Why?'
'Do not go into that, gentle knight.'
'Into the light?
'It's not the light or bitterness which ails me.' He leaned forward confidentially.
I sensed the moment had come.
'I don't want to be the lately parted,' he whispered
'The late departed? It comes to us all.'
'Not parted it doesn't.' He came closer still. 'I don't want anyone interfering
with my privacy, once I'm gone.'
'I'm sure your papers...'
'I'm not referring to them. The family jewels...' he nodded significantly,
pointing under the table. For a moment I had a vision of riches undreamed,

34

before, with a sinking sense of embarrassment, I realised the relative was indicating his crotch.

'Think of old Adam 'Three Graves' Mickiewicz. What was left of him after they'd dug him up from Istanbul?'
'Istanbul? I thought he was disinterred from Paris?'
'That was the second time. Montmorency. And now he's in Krakow. How can anyone be certain that he's.. *ALL THERE...?*'

There was a manic look in the relative's eye, and I decided desperate measures were called for.

'I'll see to it.'

I held his gaze, stronger than the basilisk, and I could see in the fading light that it was as if a great weight had been taken from my Great Uncle Dintentfass.

For the last time that day, he beckoned the waiter.

'We need a stiff one.'

The Bumper Dwarf - Wojciech Chmielewski

When the lamppost lights come on at dusk in Chłodna Street, her dark cobble-stones shine in all their former dignity. This moment is much enjoyed by the bumper dwarf who guards the gateway to one of the old tenement houses. The city, once, was full of such cast-iron bumper dwarves, two of them on every gate. It was their duty to defend the walls of tenement houses from their destruction by the axles of carts entering the courtyards and loaded with goods. The street once acted as the border of a small ghetto. From the gate of the footbridge built over it, at the command of the Germans, the bumper dwarf had a great view. He saw the city's many Jews cross this bridge in droves, and once when a bomb hit the tenement house, witnessed his twin brother dwarf perish. Here once was the teeming Jewish quarter of the city. All that remains of it today are the cobble-stones of Chłodna Street and the rail, along which trams, bearing the sign "Nur fur Deutsche" once would rattle. The bumper dwarf remembers well that notice with that sign. But that was once and once … besides, those are other tales when this one is of our times in which the dwarf is witness to a conversation taking place between Yvonna, owner of a haberdashery and Marek. her old flame from primary school. The haberdashery occupies a small establishment which you must enter from the gate. When Yvonna and Marek were in love some time ago, they'd go to the cinema and buy ice-creams, hug in the discos, kiss in the cloakrooms. But that was twenty years ago. Now Marek is a taxi-driver, while Yvonne's husband, Steven, works on a building site in England. He's been abroad for more than half a year.

"Are you closing now?" Marek asks Yvonna.

"In fifteen minutes."

"So what? Let me invite you out."

"But where to? And why?"

Yvonna, despite her thirty five years and two children, who are presently staying with a nanny, blushes a little.

"I want to show you a new bar, with karaoke, we can do a bit of singing, the food is great: kebabs, barbecue pork neck- only the best, you know."

"I'm on a diet."

"A diet- but why?" Marek raises his voice a little, "As far as I see, you haven't changed one bit. Seeing you again after these ten years...you know what? It's as if we were back in that school class-room again with all those crazy teachers. Your dancing was the best! Are you still doing it?"

"No. Well, sometimes. At weddings, for instance. But you know how rare those occasions are."

"In this bar you can even dance, there's a jukebox, you pick hits. The ones popular at our times."

"Ha! You know," Yvonne laughs and begins to draw the anti-burglar blinds in her windows, "I dreamt of you, once. It was a fairytale. During a Russian lesson you stood up and started fighting with a dragon. It had suddenly materialised and was wanting to devour me, I was really scared."

The lamp posts cast delicate light on the cobble-stones and uneven pavement. Yvonna and Marek leave the shop, Yvonna turns the alarm on and closes the door. They are still talking, but the bumper dwarf hears nothing. For a few of moments he is sound asleep, lulled by the evening music noises of Chłodna Street and his memories. So he does not learn where Yvonne and Marek went, nor what transpired that evening.

Translated by Stefan Bodlewski

Constitution Square, 6 a.m. - Jarosław Klejnocki

Here he was born. The neon light "Buy Soviet watches"
lulled him to sleep when moonlight wouldn't quite suffice;
the lights went out, the last trams bade the day goodnight.
He's back again, stranger and surprised. The candelabra
street lamps stay, though crude proletarian walls ping
ornamented now with signs flashed from another galaxy:
"The Shooters Corporation," "Phillips," "Burger King."

Almost dawn that first time did he by Hortex Restaurant
kiss her on lips in an eternal probability of June or first
days of July; arriving late, he was afraid of reprimand,
so roamed around here dreaming gates were bunkers,
the pavement a barricade, as angry by-passers scowled.

At bus stops- early morning crowd, shift-work, routine.
He's not concerned with them, a shadow, goes unseen-
He's only dropped in for a moment, no illusions felt
Well, not excessive ones, no sense of guilt.

Now the rush. The city's heart yearning for arrhythmia
This pulsar without a centre now revives, as belfries tower
over roofs of churches like those of Disneyland and Lego
Castles. His thoughts of past are deeper than foundation
stones, but weaker than so many lives. No sentiments.

The air is filled with fumes more so than mystery.
For children: fairy tales; for tourists: legends, history.
Here he was born. A good moment to confide in. A return.
But what to say about it all, and what to learn?

Translated by Stefan Bodlewski

Pani Stasia of Grochów - Wiktor Sybilski

"Hold your horses! It's not a bakery in here, you know!" Pani Stasia yells, hoping her voice will carry up the lift shaft to the fifth floor. A neighbour, impatient to descend, has been banging on the lift door. Pani Stasia appears, holding the lift door open with one hand, a cigarette in the other. Her slender figure, grey hair in a bun, sharp features, and lack of make-up give her an ominous mien. Hard to say how old she is, maybe sixty? She's chatting to the postman, revealing her secrets.

Mouth agape, I'm wondering what a bakery has in common with a lift and then I politely say "Good Morning." My neighbour scrutinizes me, searching in her mind for some excuse to slap me down. She finds it: "Dear neighbour, is it you that's crushing my head in the kitchen?! I can hear everything! Noise at three a.m.! Don't tell me I can't! I'm a professional insomniac. Radio Maria is my only solace. Except when your wooden panels begin to creak!"

Over hill, over dale, and over the Vistula River lies Warsaw's Grochow. Awake my dear reader, and allow me to let you in on some illegal information. The people of Grochów are as garrulous as London's East Enders. We have ancient customs and a Warsaw dialect, a kind of Varsovian cockney, which Polish linguists consider extinct because they're afraid to enter courtyards with tape recorders.

Anyway, just a piece of advice: if your English foot ever treads upon Grochów's green and pleasant district, remember to address the shopkeepers as "Boss," however silly that may sound, or when threatened with assault, immediately become a long-time supporter of the Legia football club, even though you know no team-members, and if you happen to meet someone, even if he is despicable, nevertheless always call him "darling."

The staircase of our pre-war tenement house, with its huge functional shape, looks menacing. Under the button of the lift opposite the entrance is a scary streak of caked brown paint, redolent of dripping blood. One day, as I am scraping it off with a screwdriver, Pani Stasia informs me: "It was that bitch who lived on the third floor before you. When she renovated her flat she spilled the paint and so it stayed!"

In the caretaker's window, gone for some time now, I put a flower. It is so much merrier. After two days, the flower's gone. I put another one. It also disappears. Pani Stasia decides to take matters into her own hands. "Did you notice, sir?! Some scumbag stole it! Now I am putting a hare's-foot fern here." After a while I place another two flowers there. Now there are three of them, but it's not long before one is gone again. Soon more and more people are discussing the matter.

Pani Kurczakowa, a neighbour who works in a nearby shop, suddenly realizes I'm a new neighbour and offers comment in a coarse voice, calling me right away by my first name, as they used to address youngsters in the neighbourhood. "See, they stole the flower, and it was so nice." Pani Stasia loses her temper: "When I catch this sodding thief! I tell you, dear neighbour, I'll...! Listen, you need to lurk on the stairs, dash down and grab him! Sometimes I sneak out onto the landing myself to see if the bastard is prowling around! I suggest you do likewise."

Soon a division of tasks comes about in the tenement house – who is well versed in electrical matters, who lends sugar, and who just asks about health or talks politics. My share is writing – for example, official letters. So I duly prepare a letter to the flower thief: "If you steal one more time – you're done for!" I was mulling over the right words to use, ones which will at once put the thief off with their bluntness, but will also be suitable for the children living in the tenement house as well as the family of Jehovah's Witnesses.

I finally pin a sheet of paper printed with an elegant font in the caretaker's window, hardly expecting it to have any effect at all. But lo and behold – the threat succeeds! The very next day, entering my flat, I notice soil scattered on the floor and a flower briskly plonked in the pot. Evidently, the thief takes pains to lurk and return the loot unseen. The whole tenement house is euphoric. The neighbour congratulates me on a successful campaign.
For some time there is peace, but soon Pani Stasia is irritated by a rag allegedly hanging from my balcony. She says, "Neighbour, my mother and I we cannot sleep at night because this rag swings in front of the window and destroys our peace of mind! Please remove it immediately!" Indeed I find on the balcony a small old dish rag and I throw it away. At last I'm invited to the neighbour's place downstairs. We are sitting in a spacious kitchen. In an old cupboard in the kitchen there are glasses indispensable to fruit liqueur. The mother and daughter tell me stories.

"Once I was drafted into the Army. On the envelope it was clearly written, 'Stanisław.' If they send it to me and the name is correct, then I take it and turn up. Why not?! But they are very surprised! And I say to them: "You drafted me, so here I am!" She pauses, adding, "Would you like some lemon

for your tea?" Then she continues, "And this thug who used to live here...,"
the mother is talking, "Mister Wiktor, when my husband was alive, the thug
made life hell for us, I couldn't open the door because he was standing there
with a knife! We wrote to the press, to television. Thirteen years to this day!"
At that, Pani Stasia loses her cool again: "Thirteen, no, make it fifteen years!"

A minor tragedy arrives: "Pani Stanisława, interrogated as a witness, con-
fessed that on 17.01.2008 she found her basement broken into and that
about 70 jars containing home-made food had been stolen." Thus the letter
from the prosecutor's office announces, which I keep as a memento in my
drawer. The thief broke into all the basements, but he stole only preserves –
marinated mushrooms, fruit preserves, and a bag to carry his loot. Soon after
the tragic incident Pani Stasia wailed, "They cleaned out the whole
basement! And I went so many times to the forest just to pick those
mushrooms!" The villain had a feast just like before the war, if you don't
mind my mentioning.... the war!

And I almost forget the ending. They lived happily ever after with the flowers
in their place and all the preserves and mushrooms standing safely on the
basement shelves. Whether in peace or economic crisis, in Poland, Russia,
England, or God forbid, in northern Dakota, home-made preserves are a very
healthy and nutritious safeguard. And you can even make lemon curd.
Whether it is from Polish lemons or not, you can store it and sleep peacefully.
As you would in Grochów.

Translated by Karolina Maślarz

Mamudov's Caravan - Jennifer Robertson

(Can warm hearts beat beneath tailored suits?

"Seven thousand miles from east to west:
seven thousand miles in heat and dust –
from Kirghizia through Kazakhstan
I ride in a gypsy caravan."
In the ministry in Warsaw officials sat mute.
Can warm hearts beat beneath tailored suits?
"From Kirghizia through green Ukraine
I follow the footsteps of Tamerlaine.
Tamerlaine brought war; my mission is peace.
I go to his monument in far Par-is.
My passport is valid – my name's Mamudov.
I ride in a wagon daubed with doves.
I invited my friend and my lad of sixteen.
We harnessed two horses, Beauty and Queen.
We stored our documents, visas and stamps,
put oats in our sacks, oil in our lamps.
We set off from home on the first of May,
travelling horse power all the way.
'Peace to the world!' I wrote on the van.
'Miru mir' in Cyrillic – read it who can!"
The Board of Agriculture shook troubled heads.
In his kaftan woven with gold and red threads
Mamudov looked – well, exotic. High hat and fur boots
contrasted strangely with high tech and grey suits.
"Look out of the window: red and gold leaves
gleam bright as the domes of ancient Kyiv.
Fifty years I saluted tyranny's flags.
Politicians wear beaver; citizens rags.
"So, seven thousand miles to the Polish border…"
'We can't let you through. Your passport's in order,
your horses are not. Go back to Brest.
Strict sanctions ban livestock imported west.'
"Rules never deter heirs of Tamerlaine!
I left my small convoy, boarded a train.
No fare was needed; they let me ride free
and directed me here. Will you help me?"
Internet access alerted Berlin.

42

"Sorry, Mamudov, they won't let you in."
"Then I'll harness myself, my son and my friend –
we will drag our van to our journey's end.
Once in Ukraine, one still summer night,
I had reason to rise, gave a robber a fright.
He could have stolen our horses, had us all killed.

He said so himself, but his kind heart prevailed."
Posteriors shifted on padded chairs.
The director spoke, "These white hairs
and my branded arm witness the wounding of war.
Let's not hinder a peace mission which has travelled so far."
Her deputy nodded, "Energy conservation, of course
What could be more ecologically sound than a horse?
I vote we help Mr. Mamudov reach the German border
by lending him horses right to the Oder."
The director continued, "Like an unwanted guest,
Tamerlaine invaded our land, laid cities to waste,
but Mamudov's nags saved peasants much toil –
seven thousand miles of fertilised soil.
"Fat cabbages, onions, beets and green beans:
what profusion for farmers where those horses have been!
My colleagues drive limousines, ride business class.
Our guest brings benevolence. I say: let him pass."
E-mails from Warsaw open the way;
Mamudov speeds on to the Champs-Elysees
with his colourful convoy; while in clover in Brest
Beauty and Queen enjoy strict sanctioned rest.

Borowski Finds His Groove - James G. Coon

Adamski exited his room at the Europejski Hotel and headed for the broad stairs spiralling down to the lobby. Passing a corner alcove, he noted the familiar figure of a man he called "the Scribe." Perched atop a lanky frame, the Scribe's shining half-dome head anchored a cascade of frizzy gray hair straining past his shoulders from the sides and back. He sported wire-rimmed glasses, heavy black leather shoes (in desperate need of polishing), a musty grayish-greenish sweater with matching greenish-grayish corduroy trousers, and a serious mien.

The Scribe hovered over an immense riot of folio papers that stretched across the coffee table and over several chairs before finally spilling onto the floor. Standing guard over this scrum of handwritten text were two weather-beaten leather satchels and an equally ancient leather book bag. A lonely cigarette of dubious provenance smouldering in an old metal ash tray completed the picture.

As Adamski rounded the corner, the Scribe looked up from his papers and nodded curtly. Adamski replied with a wink and a nod before beginning his descent to the lobby. During that short journey he pondered the curious role played by "-ego" in the Polish language and amused himself with the thought of being a "noun declining."

In due course, Adamski arrived in the lobby fully de-clenched and headed for the bar where he slowly lowered his modest bulk onto a waiting sofa. "Ahhhh," he sighed, "the body of my work has never before rested upon such a reassuringly sound and comfortable platform."

Almost immediately, the waitress arrived with his customary double espresso and mineral water with gas and placed it, along with a fresh ashtray, on the coffee table in front of him, garnishing his order, as always, with a wry grin and a wink at no extra charge. Now fully supplied, Adamski fired up a cheroot and waited patiently for the evening's show to begin.

*

It was already past twilight when Roman Borowski brushed a light dusting of snow from a bench in Łazienki Park. He had come to Warsaw hoping to rub shoulders with the nation's brightest literary lights and perhaps even become one of them. Instead, he found himself sitting on a cold park bench, enveloped by the gloom of defeat, pining for the days of the Polish Enlightenment, wondering what had gone so terribly wrong. In the end, Borowski acquiesced to the cold and the silence and steeled himself for the long slog back to his lonely room at the Europejski.

Just then he felt the bench stirring to life. The initial quiver rapidly erupted into a wild vibrating dance like the lid on a teapot about to blow. Then the back and seat of the bench pursed to form a mouth and, with a loud and slavering "PTUI!", it spit Roman into the bushes on the other side of the pathway.

"Yeach! Whaddya doin' here? Don't you know the park is closed?" the bench scolded.

"Wha..wha...wha?" Roman stammered.

"Yeah, yeah, yeah, I know.... 'O Boże, a talking bench!' Oooh...aaah... Get over it, pal, and answer my question. Whaddya doin' here?"

"I was hoping to find inspiration from the echoes of the past. Today is Thursday, is it not?"

After a moment's stunned silence, the bench opened its mouth wide and let loose a raucous horse laugh. Then, in a mincing tone dripping with sarcasm, the bench mewled,

"Oh, he wanted to avail himself of a schvitz in Lubomirski's baths and then gorge himself on King Poniatowski's food at the Thursday Dinner."

"One can always dream," Roman replied. "I've been everywhere else in Warsaw. This was my last hope."

The bench rushed at Roman and roared in his face, "As you might imagine, I've seen some sorry arses in my day, but you are the sorriest of them all. There's inspiration everywhere in Warsaw. Now get out of my park and go find it!"

With that, Roman took off running with the bench nipping at his heals like a rabid dog all the way back to the Europejski: "Uwaga! ... Woohoo! ... Klankety ... klankety ... Uwaga! Uwaga! ... Klankety ... klankety ... klank ... klank .... KLANK!"

Despite the urgency of his flight to safety, Borowski remained properly mindful of the importance of obeying the crossing lights at every intersection, sometimes running circles around cement trash bins and advertowers to evade the bench. Passers-by solemnly nodded their approval.

*

Adamski, ever the indefatigable storm chaser in the swirling maelstrom of literary trends, was in Warsaw to gather material for a follow-up to his widely admired first volume, "The Necromance of Language – A Guide to the Literature of the Future." Almost immediately, he had found nearly all the source material he needed in the lobby bar of the Europejski. Feeling satisfied that his ambitious new work, tentatively entitled "The Antic Wariat in the Modern Age," was already well underway, Adamski took a sip of his espresso and blew a smoke ring into the air.

The ring had barely formed when Roman Borowski banged through the hotel's revolving door entrance, raced into the lobby, and skidded to a halt in front of the bar. Grabbing hold with both hands, he hastily ordered a double vodka with a beer chaser, downed the first vodka and, cognizant that half measures would avail him nothing, ordered another double. From the corner of his eye, he spied Adamski motioning him to his table.

"You'll never believe what happened since we spoke at breakfast," Borowski said. Facing Adamski across the table, he accepted the offer of a cigar, lit it, downed the second vodka, and proceeded, sotto voce, to relate the entire story of the park bench.

"The bench was definitely on to something," Adamski said. "Now tell me, what did you notice most about Warsaw today?"

"Advertising! From the tall buildings swathed in canvas blankets extolling the virtues of cheap SMS messages to the advertowers encased in layers of plastered placards to the grinning windshields of parked cars involuntarily advertising burdels by the bushel, it's a never-ending anvil chorus hammering out the message to buy, buy, buy."

Not being one to let a good phallic image go to waste, Adamski nodded towards the bar and said, "See that couple?"
"You mean the middle-aged brazen hussy with the platinum blond hair and

turquoise eye-liner and the short 50-something guy who looks like a fire hydrant in a cheap suit?"

"Yes," Adamski said. "Now, tell me about them."

"The aging hussy is L.A. Suzie, the stuff of legends," Borowski offered after a brief pause.

"She does have that Los Angeles faded-glory look," Adamski said.

"Actually, the 'L.A.' stands for Legs Akimbo," Borowski said, warming to the subject. "During the Cold War she worked in the service of a friendly Western nation. Since embassy personnel were prohibited from fraternizing with locals, all the strapping young soldiers attached to the embassy flocked to her bedroom. Every night the entire apartment block could hear them singing a rousing chorus of that old Jimmy Durante standard, 'There Are Two Sides to Every Girl.'"

"Good lord, the mere thought wilts my lettuce!" Adamski cried out.

"But her salad days ended along with the Cold War, and the daily drumbeat on her bedroom door ceased. With the help of a small trust fund, she soon took early retirement and has been working the hotel lobbies of Warsaw ever since, posing as a career counselor."

"Now you're cooking!" Adamski cheered.

"The diminutive fire hydrant is Terrance Hoggswallup Ugo, better known on the street as Thugo, until recently a Big Dog in the financial world. Markets would rise and fall with his every howl, but over the past few years his fortunes have waned substantially. Now, far from being a Big Dog, Thugo is just another wan cur on his way to the pound."

"Excellent! Now let's listen in on their conversation, already in progress," Adamski said.

"Speaking as Warsaw's pre-eminent career counselor, you look like a man desperately in need of a really good job," Suzie said, using her standard opening gambit.

"You got that right, lady! I was making big money before they accused me of reporting false profits. Picky, picky, picky. Even Bush said that profits are just opinions, so I'm entitled to mine, right?"

"No man is a prophet in his own land," she said, "but that's just my opinion."

"And it appears that I have missed all the good bubbles, even here – real estate, dodgy stocks, and the złoty. What's a good old wide boy to do?"

"Thugo, you have come to the right place. It just so happens that my specialty is stiffening the resolve of job seekers so they can cut the mustard in the dog eat hotdogi world of contemporary Warsaw."

"And what do you propose?"

"You need a brand new shtick, slick, something that combines your ability to spin a plausible tale with your talent for producing short change. In cases such as yours, I normally recommend becoming a Professional Quant, but it seems that you have already exhausted that route."

"Sadly, yes. For years I received high praise for being a Professional Quant, but when those same people see me now, the only thing they can say is 'See You Next Tuesday.' Somehow, it doesn't carry the same caché."

"Not to worry," Suzie said. "I know of a very big hole in the Polish market that needs filling immediately. The job is yours for the asking." Then Suzie whispered in Thugo's ear, "The Duża Dzura of Dzisiaj is ...."

".... satire!" Borowski exulted discretely. Adamski nodded sagely as the bumptious beat of a bongo bopped over Borowski's banter...

... boppedy ... boppedy ... bop ... bop ... boppedy ... BOP ... BOP ... BOP!

... drawing all eyes and ears to a man, dressed entirely in black, standing next to a piano, holding a flashlight that illuminated his face from below.

"It's Krebski, the great slam poet," everyone whispered in awe, especially impressed by his carefully groomed Van Dyke beard. Once the entire lobby had grown silent, Krebski furiously declaimed his latest poem of protest, "Speaking Japolski," to the beat of an atonal slam piano accompaniment.

Ami Wami
Fuji Jama
Jaki Taki To

Ego Emu
Hiro Hito
Taki Po Co To

Hara Kiri
Honda Nissan
Jaki No To Co

In a melodramatic gesture, Krebski ended his poem by assuming the crucifix posture and waiting for applause, which came like rapturous thunder from three skateboard-toting teenagers wearing baseball caps backwards. Taking advantage of the distraction, Suzie and Thugo took French leave.

"And finally," Adamski asked Borowski, "who is that man driving the piano?"

"That's Michał 'The Cat' Miał, whose boffo one-man show at the Bufo Theatre, 'All Cats Speak Polish,' featuring his retro Boogie-Woogie hit, 'Kup Mi Mamo, Eight to the Bar,' is all the rage amongst the sushi suckers."

"The winds of a great afflatus have truly filled your sails, my friend," Adamski intoned. "Now sally forth and bring a salubrious snap of the Borowski towel to the posteriors of an eagerly awaiting public." As Borowski hurried off, Adamski cried out after him, "May the farce be with you always!"

*

Back in his room, Adamski found an envelop containing several handwritten pages resting serenely on his pillow. At the top of the first page he read, "Adamski exited his room ...." Adamski smiled, placed the pages back in the envelop, and carefully filed it along with the rest of the Scribe's submissions.

On Ujazdowskie - Judith Eydmann

Stepping out onto the tidy viaduct
an infantile geometry gestates behind the eyes
this foreigner in a place unpronounceable
reading the stately roads.

I had to leave the gardens
because you were not there to help me
and unable to read the translations
I fumbled through the spavined arteries
stumbling on scientific names.

It was unexpected
that desire would be this militant
that time well spent
with those who know the world
could not assuage my hunger.
The howl returns, riding my shoulder
back to the house of insolvent ruins.

Seeking silence in the many spaces
on they play, the waste sonatas.
I must be further adrift in the Universe
flying at a different speed
from the rows of rested people
reclining in deckchairs
arms folded.

Aparat - Ben Borek

With Slings and Arrows

Aparat had bought himself a new,
citrus-infused tobacco. I had told him
not to do it. That the stuff was too cheap
to be of any value. He then pulled
a grin from out his pocket. I translate:
it said, "I favour that of equilibrium.
I favour that more doctored, more at ease,
within itself. Without itself as well."
He slopped around his bald soliloquy.
I offered him a change of scenery.
Let's walk the Warsaw lines. Let's take
a tramwaj, or the pavement, let's become
another duo in a photograph.
I cannot speak of his redundant laugh.

At the sex-strip by Plac Grzybowski

And if he saw a flighty bird
it codified his flight. He fled.
He has to keep a sort of even head
and keep his thoughts from being overheard.
The chatter in the naked autumn light
is all of traffic and a slushy tongue.
The light is blue and it is brown
and verdigris between where sky meets town.
The strip of booths is red, but faded, blanched
by time-abuse and elements and such.
It isn't much to look at but, look in,
beyond the traffic and the petrol din.
Yes, that's the point! His head tumesces. Run!
Go! Aparat, your coins are quite enough
to pay the man and watch a bit of stuff.

Around Koło - Andrew Fincham

It's not possible to avoid history in Warsaw; it sits on every street corner: the city is paved from it. Not that remote version of history which echoes round ancient ashlars, unfolding with the delicate decay of an ivied tower. Savagery and chivalry notwithstanding, Warsaw's is a history of death. Death for thousands and hundreds and tens of thousands of men and women, children and babies, raised by fire and bombings and bullets and by lethal blows against brick walls.

Warsaw is built from those same bricks. And all along the walls, on streets as wide as socialist realism, and on those narrower than fate, stand little monuments in slate and ever-darkening bronze. They flower for a few of the life-sized heroes whose deeds (and deaths) took place there half a century ago. This is the history of the mind – we can remember them. If you were not alive under the occupation, then your mother will remember. If Grandmother cannot remember, it is because she is dead.

Yet little by little it fades away along with the people who remember the September campaign and the Uprising, and the Ghetto and the Transportations. New plaster and paint smooth the scars which once marked every building left standing. Now the developers and the grants wash away these mementi mori before our eyes, until soon they will be no more. And then it will be the time for monuments to serve, and we will know that we have forgotten.

But for those who like to take a little piece of history home, there is still a place where the memories of the city come to die. You need to get up early to catch the best – they evaporate easily in the morning sunshine. For the market at Kolo draws punters from far and wide, beckoning the dealers and the dealt, the shyster and the shark, all with a view to moving on memories and parting with them for a price. As in flea markets everywhere, the tourist provides the life-blood of Kolo. Yet because there are so many tourists, and Grandmas tend to live longer every year, the old memories don't appear quite as often as they used to. The stall holders and the cheapjacks are hard pushed to create enough to satisfy demand. That may be why it is only held two days a week – to give the Witkacy's time to dry. It wasn't so long ago I was driving home trying to trace a smell of fresh paint unnoticed in the open air when I'd paid a chancer's price for a small oil by Leon Wyczółkowski: the books claim he died in 1936. For historians of memories, there's no need to buy museum quality works at fast food prices. These are a small portion of the selection, and best kept for the vain.

A car park during the working day, the market spreads over a couple of acres of blacktop in low rise heaps, the wares creating alleys by their absence, laid out on sheets of plastic or an occasional trestle. There are three kinds of stall at which you can try your luck: if it's not junk or Jewish then it's something to do with the Germans and death. Pick your way through the sea of rusting enamel, old locks, and tables with three legs shorter than the fourth, and you will find silverware gleaming red-gold in the early autumn sun, reflecting shadows on faded velvet, like over-zealous altars.

The Jewish stuff is semi-historic, if not anachronistic; it is there simply because people expect it to be there. You'd have to believe every single one of Poland's four million murdered sons of Abraham smuggled a couple of candlesticks out of the ghetto for so much to appear every week. Perhaps they did. Some believe it still.

But silver is for marking wedding anniversaries and retirements, for making memories of one's own, better than reading another's reflections. It's too impersonal, too easily melted down and reformed, and too happy to take the imprint of another life; especially after it has been polished.

But it is in the other third where you find the nuggets of true history. Veteran trophies of war, scratched water bottles and holy helmets, scarred by a rifle bullet behind the temple; officers' pocket watches and hundreds of medals, each with the arachnidine swastika nestling in its centre or crawling over the top. This is what makes the history hawks come here for their slice of Warsaw's past. They are the collectors, seeking another member for their cabinets of war.

The piece de resistance, the apex of reality on top of the tree, must be the Nazi dagger. Most desirable of all to conduct that frisson so essential when handling historic horror, is the black and silver blade worn by the officer elite of the SS. To handle such a weapon, draw its lethal edges out into the open, touch the needle point, and weigh life in the balance – surely no other reality comes near. At any rate, daggers (even those dew-fresh from the workshops in Wola) fetch the highest prices. And I almost bought one.

I'd drawn a blank that morning, wandering, and wondering whether there was anything I could find that I needed. Still, the air was crisp and I'd needed an excuse to get up. I was wondering whether I also needed a reason to pay six beer's worth for a wooden tool box with AK scratched on the side (to show it had served the resisting home Armia Krajowa), and I did.

The vendor, to give the fellow a title, seemed not at all anxious to part with it, but it was hard to see why. He sat in a corner outside the market proper, leaning against a wall on the one side and hemmed in on the other by a large canvas-backed lorry owned by one of the more professional operators. Apart from the box, his meagre collection consisted of a broken toaster and a picture of the Black Madonna, cut from a book and askew in a warped frame, all artfully arranged on a dismal tartan blanket.

I had a decreasing desire to spend any more time on the discussion: the price would already get him comfortable on vodka for a couple of days. I was beginning to doubt the authenticity of the box (I still do), and was fingering the grooves, not having the heart to mention that his scratch-marks looked dubious. Then, giving me a keener glance than his walnut face had seemed capable, he leaned confidentially forward.

'You know the war.' It was statement, rather than a question, but I nodded, anyway. 'I fight with AK. In Warsaw army.' His face was close to mine, and I held my breath. Obviously. 'I show you something.' He reached within the upper layers in which he was wrapped, drawing out a roll of newspaper which he began to unfold. It was a compelling performance, perhaps one he had given many times before, but it held the attention: all the excitement of 'Pass the Parcel,' with its concomitant risk of disappointment. The opened bundle displayed a double-edged knife: a dagger, one should say. It was stained red brown with rust, the nickel slightly flaking on the cross-guard, with a kink in the blade. Only the insignia button gleamed on the ebonised wood, rubbed smooth with years of handling. The angular letters of the SS button above an eagle clasping the Nazi spider. I reached out to pick it up, but the package withdrew rapidly back to his breast.

'Not for touching. Not for selling. For telling.' And this is what he told:

He had been in the uprising for thirty two days. There was not much to live off, but always something. The hardest part was the thirst. He had come to Warsaw from the north, from Gdynia, brought up in the country, with a farm wagon sending milk into the city every day. But he had drifted towards the capital for safety, and waited until it was time to fight and the sky went black with smoke and red with fire and stayed like that for eight days until the wood had burned out and the fallen walls were mined and the cellars turned into hospitals and hideaways. He did not say anything about the fighting. There was a boy who wouldn't stay down, and they had waited twelve hours to carry him down to the dressing station because he had been hit in the morning in the full sunshine of an early September day. The boy had not cried much, but he had stayed with him when they removed his leg, and was still with him when the boy died early the following morning. This was halfway through the fight, and before the city was being torn down block by block. Then the position was overrun and five wounded men sat with him in a cellar, listening to the end of the battle for the old town.

A rattle on the steps, and the enemy appeared: he was no longer young, too tall for his uniform, with the face of a Jew. He wore the insignia of the Totenkopf, and was drunk with more than the fight. Most of the wounded wore uniforms from the SS stores in Wola, overrun in the first few days of the rising, and this caused confusion. But not for long. With inebriated care, documents were checked, and death pronounced. Each man was executed, the blade precisely into the throat. But the man from Gdynia was luckier: the SS man was a Danziger, perhaps one who had beaten the Polish customs men in the months before the war, disguised as sporting tourists. Theirs was a reunion, and a bottle of medical spirit was taken in bruderschaft. By the time night fell, the death's head had been joined by half a dozen more, and had fallen asleep embracing his fellow Pomeranian. Apart from the one set to watch, the others followed. There was to be no more fighting there that day.

The blood from the dying men was perhaps still wet when the man from Gdynia drew the blade gently from its scabbard, and with utmost care silently pushed it into the neck of the man sleeping on his shoulder. With equal decision, he had moved amongst the silent men, and made each die within the silence of a nauseous gurgle. Then he edged up the stair to find the guard gone, and so ran into the burning night.

He had wiped the blade on his sleeve, and the dagger was still in his hands. The steel held engraved words, stained by rust:

Meine Ehre heist Treue.

My honour is loyalty – a two-edged sword.

I came round, disturbed. I'm pretty sure he asked me for money for a taxi, to take me and show me the place. I may have given him a fifty, and tried to explain he should stay there whilst I fetched my friend, who could ask much better questions in his native Polish than

I returned in less than ten minutes, but could not at first find his corner: Koło is like that. I eventually recognised the canvas of the lorry, and hurried round the back. There was nothing there. Not even a space to place a blanket.

That's what Kolo is like.

But when they open up a cellar in the old town, and find the bones of five Poles and five Germans, all marked by the same knife, I shall have a story to tell.

And I've still got the box.

News from Puławska - Maria Jastrzębska

Spring's so late;
the storks flew in last week.
Snows have melted too fast:
trees stand knee-deep in floods.
Buds are small, skies milky grey.
Only the mistletoe glistens
like balls of green string
hung in brown trees.
Political jokes are back:
Radio Maryla blaring out loud
to the mohair beret brigade
even the Vatican was embarrassed.
The air smells of mud.
You can hear hymns playing;
a spokesman denies instances.
We've had record sales
of pussy willow. Whatever happens
our strawberries will be best -
you have to eat them straight away
or they turn to mush –
not like those grown to look red
or withstand long lorry rides.
If summer ever comes
ours will still be the sweetest.

Evolution - Sławomir Shuty

At the beginning the training was a nightmare. He wondered if it had all been worth it. Whether the compulsory work undertaken, the painstaking training exercises, would really deliver the promised, long-awaited job fulfilment and financial satisfaction. In the maze of frustrating procedures it was hard to be at your constant best. In frequent moments of doubt he thought of resigning forthwith, burning his bridges, ditching his references from data bases. He craved to give in to emotions, to act spontaneously and listen to the voice of intuition. In a word, he was in a grim mood. And the conditions?

God forbid. Did he expect them to be so bad. It was beyond his imagination that the employers cared so much for their staff but not for him. With a sense of helplessness he complained whenever he could. So what? Nobody took him seriously. It was a tough school of hard knocks. The point was the cage was awfully cramped.

To tell the truth, he wasn't able to stretch his limbs. The back got used to being hunched, his hands hanged torpidly, limply beside the torso. His legs were bent. Curled up, he fell asleep, unaware of dangers lurking in the dark. The least advantage to being in a cage. Every morning he received fresh water and a bowl filled with leftovers. Hay was changed every week, which he managed to quickly muck up in time. Slowly, he learned to excrete his bodily fluids outside the cage, so the bed remained dry for a longer period. To go outside even for a moment was out of the question. Well, he knew what he had chosen. Only one thing to do; stick it out.

He would hang suspended from the upper bars of the cage for hours. His huge jaws chewed raw meals, rotten carrots, musty onions, foul meat. He bombarded the inquisitive onlookers gathered around the cage with marrowless bones. He spat on the smiling faces and stuck his bottom in the air to the amusement of the mob.
After some time he realized that when he is nice, he gets candy from them. He decided to work on that and it produced the desired effect.

Slowly, he attained excellent interpersonal skills and treated the visiting guests very kindly. He easily made eye contact with them. From the onlookers amused with his frolics, he took tasty bananas, which became his delicacy and thanked them politely. He was gallant to women, while to children – delicate. However, he still grinned at the specimens of the same sex. Although from a distance it could have looked like a failed attempt to smile. He wiped his bottom with the left hand, while the right one was stretched out, always as the initiator, in the gesture of welcome. He introduced himself at the beginning of a conversation and precisely remembered the name of his interlocutor. His vocabulary expanded with lots of precious words used in the world of business. Also his countenance changed. While his figure straightened up, the skin became brownish, delightfully tanned, biceps rounded in a very appealing way. He willingly decided to remove hair in intimate places.

He treated women with respect and a visible professional reserve, which excluded him from the circle of suspects known for improper behaviour in the workplace. Sexist practices, furtive glances on the bust, comments on the curves of buttocks were out of the question. Nothing of the kind, in a word he was fully professional and became an expert in the most important political problems of the world. He could correctly pinpoint trouble spots on the map, which could become the hotbed of armed conflicts. He used two hands and all pieces of cutlery to consume his meal. He read this and that. He got the knack that he lacked.

The patrons were pleased with his progress during the training, since it indicated that the money invested in the employee had not been squandered. His new conditions were commensurate with the results. The fodder improved. Among the sticky slush, sweet raisins appeared. Used baggy clothes were replaced with designer suits. The austere cage changed into a refined apartment. The smell of sweat was masked with an expensive mixture of fragrances composed in the best laboratories. His sporty figure combined exquisitely with the luxurious interiors and exclusive cars. The branded cigar and a glass of good wine suited him. In order to achieve the utmost expertise he spent hours on swimming in the deep water, practised blows below the belt and through torturing rodents, he got rid of human emotion. The most important thing in this profession was to keep a cool head. Success did not come easily. He has to remember it every day. This life is not all roses. Only a hard butt, strong elbows, and a soft nape guarantee promotion.

He passed the exam crowning the training with distinction: good manners, negotiation skills, creativity, the ability to work in a team and in stressful conditions – all at the highest level.

He regarded the stages with some fear, since the higher you climbed, the easier it was to fall . But there was no turning back. Nor will there be.

Translated by Katarzyna Waldegrave

Identity - John a'Beckett

Ruminating as I stomp in shoe-look boots through powder snow
down once war-blistered partly patched up Mokotowska Street,
Satisfied to smile upon another month, year, century and now
a whole millennium gone by. Happy to remain a flat non-entity,

I'm damned if I can understand this current industry of our Identity
especially now the Cold War's over. Every Polish citizen I meet
is carrying a "Dowód Osobisty". It seems being born some place

and time and by a mother with a maiden name is not enough-
You have to prove it. What is this Gothic ghost we hunger-chase,
to be certain we're the person that we are - or meant to be?

Am I to believe leaves - blown in my face, I notice, by the breeze's
whiff - are passports to the foliage of trees? Branches with visas!
Mind you, my students'll be damned if they'll ever sit for an exam
But, man, they'll kill for a certificate which says they can

"Speak it" so much they'll stand in a drab and long, dank queue
for a stamp in "English" in their books which proves authentically
to the University of Bollocks they can say things like "Thank you."

Say, Cicero, even to some codger that we "intimately know,"
those everyday encounters that we have, the million meetings:
do we need our arses branded by The Ministry For Greetings
in order that we get permission now to say things like: "hello"?

Romek and Juliasia - A. Bo

Dear Ben,

Sorry I couldn't make it to The Journalists Dinner last November. Grażyna and I were busy making wedding preparations with church and family. So many documents requested by the marriage bureau! About which I'll ask you later, but now Graż and I will tie the knot in late July for eternal conjugal bliss, and you and Bożena are, of course, top of the list of invitees to the reception. What I did want to button-hole you about over drinks at the Dinner was to boast I took your tip and followed up with that Sports Writer job for The Gazette. I did the interview, got the job, I'm happy at Gazette and football reporting's proving to be a real kick.

At "Warsaw Planet" you were a tough Daily Editor, but you were right. "Not bad reporting, Bodo. But... !" you'd always say. That crashing "But.. !" of yours! No, "Planet" wasn't for me. All that paranormal stuff about sightings, revenants, and reincarnations, not my forte. So when you briefed me last January to cover the "Lovers from Verona Surface" story, I frankly thought you'd gone plain nuts. Alright, so a few New Age types have had hallucinations of a Varsovian Rom and Julie - that doesn't make it news. Or so I concluded as I traipsed down the city's empty back streets on my way to my favourite pub to mull over my next career move. Indeed I was about to laugh your whole assignment in the face when a romantic shout billowed out of neighbouring Szniadecki Street:

"Ah, you - my beloved -- Juliasia!"

Now it's my turn to go nuts, I thought. Or was my guilty conscience over rejecting your brief taking on the vox humana? A short doubting moment and I shrugged it off. After all, there are many chics in Warsaw called "Juliasia." Then, singing above the humdrum boom of traffic and its distant squeal of police sirens I heard:

"You, Romek of my dreams?!"

Here I'll make a part admission, Ben. While it's true I don't believe in revenants, I will run with co-incidence. After all, you get that in football, too. In short, curiosity got the better of me, enough to double back down the archway and peek my head around the corner. Well, damn if it wasn't Shakespeare's Sat-fated lovers trysting in the moonlight! Warsaw being short on spacious balconies, they were standing outside a small beer-bar called "Prawdziwy"("The Genuine"). The rest of the street was obscured by the gateway arch.

I stood there thinking to myself, "Could Ben be right?" But, wait a minute, moonlight at 5 pm? Just then, as I was expecting this Romek voice to proclaim, "And, you my sweetest, Juliasia...," what I got was a curt ...

"And—cut!", coming through a megaphone and promptly followed by:

"Hey, lovers, that was fantastic! But....."

It was the "But..." that did it, Ben. I promptly turned on my heels. Doubling back down the archway, I found I'd walked into a film production. My view of the lovers was blotted out by an obese director in a peaked cap addressing them. Was Michael Moore about to give us one from the heart? I wondered.

"A great take, lovers. Bee-yoooteeful. But ... I just wanna get you to sex the cherry a bit, know what I mean? Could we do it again with a bit of foreplay, you know, erotyczny?"

The Putative Lovers from 15th Century Verona looked at each other with asphyxiating incomprehension and then stared vacantly back at the director as if he were a misguided angel.

"Was that a "'yes'?" he asked. "It was? Super. So, from the top again, lovers. Take two: Sexy. Lights-camera-action!"

How dumb I'd been. You'd simply wanted me to cover the making of a 2009 Rom-and-Julie Movie. Forget career moves, Bodo, I told myself, you're back on the job again. Instinctively I pulled out my note pad on the chance of an interview with Michael Moore, if only it weren't for those noisy sirens!

A police van screeched to a halt and a bunch of cops trundled out, interrupting Take Two I might add, and then, natychmiast, they arrested the entire film crew, director, and cast for making erotic movies without a license. I take it they were from the Warsaw Vice Squad. There was a rumble of protest, but it was brought to a halt by one of the more burly cops shouting:

"Get into the van or I'll wreck the lot of you!"

With everyone briskly bundled into the van, it sped off into Centrum bearing our two Lovers to their judicial fate. I was left thinking: what is Love these days but a mere edited piece of celluloid on the cutting room floor in the unfinished and endless movie of our existence.

Which brings me to those marriage documents I need, Ben. You and Bozena have threaded the needle in this bloody marriage protocol business, so maybe you can help me. You see, I need a witness to the fact that I'm not already married. Now, you've known me for years, Ben, and I was wondering if you might oblige?

Anyway, pre-empting your cooperation in this matter, I duly dragged myself down to The Ministry For Cordial Affairs in Crow Street and joining the queue I'll be damned if among the lost souls waiting outside the grey building I didn't spy the Lovers from Verona, continuing their exchange of vows:

"And you Juliasia, your eyes, your lips, your words."
"And you, Romek, you need only be and....."

"And you're both applying for Permission to Conduct an On-Going Relationship, are you? Lovely. Do you have an Affection Certificate?" asked a cordial woman from the Ministry, carrying a folio.

An Affection Certificate? Rom and Julie looked at her then back at each other as if they were two time-warped characters trapped in The Twilight Zone.

"Well, I'll see what I can do," the lady continued. "Meanwhile, The Ministry would be grateful if you could furnish us with a Love License, Proof of Devotion, a Letter of Infatuation, and, of course, a Romantic Mission Statement. Could you follow me, please?"

And do you know, Ben, as our two misfiled lovers were ushered into the grey building on sunny Crow Street, the air suddenly became thick with questionnaires. A storm began to brew, clouds of documents stacked up into a thick folio, and after a lightening flash from the celestial photo-copying machine and a thunder of rubber stamps, it started raining application forms! And I was left thinking: "What is Love but a mere document in the ever-rolling filing cabinet of our human existence?"

Alright, Ben, calm down and I'll come to my beef. While you've been away at your mental health resort, the ad-bombardment of Warsaw I mentioned the last time we met has reached a new mountainous height. There's hardly a building left standing that isn't covered with huge advertisement hoardings. The reklamas are coming at us left, right, and centre.

So, you'll be pleased to know, a secret Overground Advert-Resistance Movement has begun. To avoid detection, its members talk to one another in the coded language of advertisements. Many young people are joining the Movement. I was coming out of the metro only the other day when lo and behold, if it wasn't our Verona Lovers, once again, exchanging their sweet nothings:

"Tired of saying...Oh, Romek...! Try saying... Hi, Juliasia!"
"Yes! Purchase your "Hey, Romek! – Hi Juliasia"—now!"
"It's the only greeting. And no charge for the introduction!"
"Available on all street corners. You and value-added Me."
"You-and-Me! There's no one like Us. Instant recovery guaranteed!"
"Want answers? Try asking...questions! Right now I'm asking:
'"Where's the next meeting?'" and I'm loving it."
"Try Marek's at 6 - you'll be so glad you came."
"I'll see you there, then. "Bye"
"Yes, why don't you try parting with...Bye!" It's on the tip of...
"..just about everyone's tongue. Buy Bye! - and buy it -- Now!"

And off they sped. I chased after them but was somehow pulled in the opposite direction by those irresistible market forces of consumerism. Drawn back into the Underground (I wish I meant the Movement and not the metro), it wasn't long before I was swallowed up by the omnipresent swirl of consumer goods and left standing on Centrum platform thinking: What is love but a mere commercial in the unending soap-opera of our human lives?

Ben, just take it easy and I'll come to my point. Your psycho-therapist is right. We're so wired up to the Present these days, with all this cell-phone, lap-top technology, we need to take a break from the whole network and immerse ourselves in the Past. So, after a stressful day's reporting last month, I decided to lose myself in the Middle Ages by escaping to the Stare Miasto. I mean, you get a feeling in the Old Town that you're back in the Renaissance. Well, I wasn't long strolling round Plac Zamkowy before I saw the Lovers from Verona for real, in their element. This time there was no interference from the rat race. They were back where they came from, in the 15th Century.
"I see you now, Romek, and the world and its time disappears,"

"In your sight, Juliasia, the seconds turn into infinite years,"
"The world and its time may tear us apart,"
"You remain, every beat, every call in my heart,"
"When you are here all the noise of the city departs,"
"And I hear the music of our two beating hearts..."

And suddenly there was harmony in the skies, as the shining satellite-studded heavens of information jingled with a glorious combination of Rick Wagner's Tristan and Isolde and Lenny Bernstein's "Tonight" from Westside Story. Heavenly music bouncing off the wing-discs of angel-satellites and softly descending into the tiny speakers of the lovers' individual cell-phones. And the grace, Ben, with which our sat-struck couple, turning briefly away from one another so that the angelic voices would come within network range, plucked their cell-phones out of their chest pockets, and raised them to their ears...

"Romek here...slucham...hallo...tak-tak-tak-tak....cholera!..."
"Juliasia on the line...No crap...shoot it at me...fire away..!"
"...Have you shifted that stuff yet?!...Well it's got to move..."
"What?!.. I can't believe this....Tell 'em I want it now...Kurda!"
"Spare me the bull about crises, koreks, queues, murder!"
"This is a pain...no, not 'at the end of the day,' ..yesterday!"
"No, I can't hold on, I'm effing in love ..Daj mi spokój!"
"Well tell him to get out of love and get busy. I'm outa here!"
"Do papa. Czeszcz! Over and out!"

And it was then, Ben,that they approached each other with fixed eyes and just before embracing hurled their cell-phones over their shoulders, over the terrace of Plac Zamkowy, and walked arm in arm toward the sunset, whispering sweet nothings in each others' ears, so much in love it was as if Warsaw didn't exist.

Their discarded cell-phones, hitting the street beneath, triggered a series of electrical short-circuits and the whole city began exploding with joy. Ben, it was like the Millennium Sylwester, the Fourth of July! Lights burst on in otherwise dark trams, dead kiosks suddenly came to life. Nuns took flight, drunks froze in rapture and staring skywards let their vodka bottles slip from their grasp and crash onto the pavement. Church-bells furiously peeled. Statues came alive. Stanczyk the court jester began rattling his bell-cap, Mickiewicz and Chopin winked. The Mermaid slipped down from her pedestal and, flinging her sword into the Vistula, began kissing everyone in sight. Marshal Piłsudski raised his bowed head and shouted "Go for it!" King Sigismund leapt off his column and raced after Romek, shouting "'ll get that boy!" The Pied Piper of Konstancin pranced out of the bowels of the Palace of Culture and Science, followed by a dancing train of midget businessmen, then joined by the entire population of the city linking arms and dancing as they hurled their cell-phones onto the pavements and crushed them under their heels.

And the lovers, oblivious of the ecstatic chaos, walked on into the Slavonic Twilight whispering sweet nothings in each other ears. I was left thinking: "If only Ben were here, and not with his psycho-therapist, he'd discover what Love really is." You should've been here, Ben. It was quite something.

Bodo

The Idiot - Leo Yankevich

Whenever I sit with the village idiot,
it's always with genuine reverence and a bit
of suspicion. Usually we just stare at the rooks,
and he sips my beer without asking, then looks
deranged as if to say he's sorry. He knows enough
about me to know I like diamonds in the rough.
And, strangely, he and I always notice the same things:
hieroglyphs in the snow, tiny holes in our fillings.
When he's not around, my wife says he's a blackguard
and a parasite, a charlatan, and a drunkard;
and I try to explain that he's just the village idiot,
and that once in a while it's necessary to sit
with him and share a pint. Later, when she falls asleep,
out of pity and out of love, I allow him to sneak
into her bed and fondle her thin white thighs,
and, if she doesn't protest, to spend the night.

The Carpet Beaters - James G. Coon

I live in a nation of carpet beaters.
even in winter I hear them
in the courtyard
beating their
carpets with their
carpet-whackers

whomp whomp whomp.

in Spring it is a major cause of
air pollution.
an entire nation of city-dwelling
carpet beaters
whacking their dust
into the air.

the wind carries the dust
into my apartment and
soon I'll be out there
beating my carpet with the
best of them.

We all need something to look
forward to in life.

Market forces, Polish-style - Jennifer Robertson

Small stalls spread wide, traders thrive.
I relish such carefree commerce, dive
readily into this teeming hive;

buy honey supplied by bountiful bees,
sorrel, young beets, soft white cheese.
The stall-holder's stores of smiles increase.

She weighs out laughter, a bright carillon.
Her face is red, a radiant plum –
she outshines the sun!

Her daughter pushes a covered pram,
'Pancakes, pancakes, soft and warm!
Make your mouth water, fresh from the flame!'

She yodels on. Heads turn. Folk stare.
'First time I hear someone sing their wares
since the years, I'm sure, before the war.'

'Before the war - that was poverty!
Look at us now: what luxury!
Pancakes, pancakes, buy two, buy three!'

Do they mean, I wonder, the war
which blasted this market square:
terror's five year grim nightmare?

Or the nine times five years of planned retail
when anyone with anything for sale
struck up a whispered deal?

Markets were closed, alleyways ill-lit,
unappetising fare issued by the state
with no song to sing, no tale to relate,

nor anything to advertise
except statistics the nation knew were lies.
So yes: 'Pancakes, pancakes...' takes us by surprise,
produce of home-grown enterprise.

Wrong number - John a'Beckett

Out of a shimmering city noon
crowd-thick and traffic-heavy,
its individual noises pampered to a groan,
on busy Świętokrzyska Street, a public phone
rings, bellows loud its ringing
cutting through the drone
as if to make a trance of it.

But no one answers it.

The granite patience of my Poles.
Everything about this phone
among the others queued for,
cards pushed in, dialled, spoken into, so alone
disappears into disbelief, the acceptance stone
and life-long lesson where we learn
to live with every still-existent thing

including its persistent ring.

Who can this caller be?
Some silenced conscience suddenly let free?
The answer to a prayer
half-prayed but meant to reach
now washed up drift-wood
on this people-pebbled beach?
Then, from some grand malaise, the tonic

now transformed, gone telephonic?

Or some trapped message now
in blinking fits at three,
short of a receiver and unfit to bear
the pressing silence cracked,
has gone for the last call
and in this deafening glare,
hit the jugular and called from there

up anyone from anywhere?

Thinking it's for me
But somehow knowing that it is:
some clandestine friend and his
following my movements,
I pick it up, put the mouth-piece cup
to my lips and let forth in gaps
"a'Beckett here!" but he, perhaps
knowing that it is me just...

hangs up.

Pterodactylus - Paula Gutowska

We're staring up at the high clock dial under the spire of The Palace of Culture. It's four o'clock, hour of the dreamlike crowds. The metro rumbling under us like a tom-tom drum, a pogo-dance at a gig.

"You shouldn't take the pitcher to the table, Madame, the milk is for everyone".

The waitress wears green beads and is a little cross-eyed. Nearby, the Chilean musicians who came once to my city to study and then stayed on are dancing, drumming, hammering out their tunes, evoking ghosts as they wave their blunt hatchets or play the pan-flute. Rain pours from the sun like a meteor but there is no rainbow. The street painter duly covers her paintings with a plastic wrap. Her works are neither wild nor crazy, ginger, filled with holey cheese; devoid of anger. Yet, in the Palace there was a Dali exhibition of giraffes on fire and cupboards, intriguing us with a mysterious evil emanating from them in a marijuana stupor. The painter makes us see these restless eyes, hazel, green and deep, hundreds of them in the shops of Empik. A nervous man is rattling his umbrella and a blonde girl whose make-up is so thick it almost creates an Event Horizon. Some Annie Someone calls to another: impatiently they are waiting for their Internet Sweethearts and so go searching for a yellow spotted T-shirt, red baseball cap and yesterday's crumpled newspaper in the thickening crowd; a clandestinia of signs. They hide their disappointment when their Chosen One turns out to be a merry, uninhibited old man.

It's getting dark. Silence moves in deceitfully as if it were a rider on a panther. It overtakes the pre-war tenement houses (from which the young insurgents of the Uprising would surface at the "W" hour). The Golden Terraces and the PKiN. The tablet with Stalin's name is overgrown with dirty moss. The stone barefoot workers smile gloomily at the housing estates as long as a grey sleep, overwhelmed by the colours of hotels and burger booths. The rider believes Warsaw is like a woman's soul: eclectic, varied and as tangled as the many threads in the hands of an absent-minded weaver of fate. The rider casts a northern shadow on the clock and disappears down the back streets as Nowy Świat flares up with swarms of rebellious glow-worms. Cafe life simmers down. A musician from the barbican takes out his violin and scatters small change disturbing the peace. When nothing plays anymore, nothing creaks. Pairs of lovers and a madman stroll around the Old Town. The madman is bald. Clad in a long coat and high-heeled shoes, he clenches his teeth and runs. But when he has also disappeared around the grey corner, a wild pterodactylus spreads out its black wings over my Warsaw.

Translated by Karolina Maślarz and John a'Beckett

The New Colossus - James G. Coon

Unlike the Bully Broad of Anglo-Saxon fame,
Whose sloshing thighs smother the charred land,
Here on our parked-car windshields shall stand
A scorching beauty with surging bust, whose flame
Is rampant lust incarnate, and her name
Mother of Exiles. With her beaconing hand
She welcomes you inside; her wild eyes command
The love-starved pilgrim to ascend her frame.
"Keep, Anglo-World, your freeze-dried lump!" cries she
With pulsing hips. "Give me your tired, your bored,
Your curdled messes yearning to live free,
The retching refugees from your whining shore,
Send these, the loveless and drought-parched, to me:
I lift my red lamp o'er the unmarked door."

Portrait - Jennifer Robertson

Zofia Nałkowska: the writer as an old woman

Her genius acclaimed when she was just fifteen,
she rises now at dawn, opens shop, trades
tobacco. Hostess par excellence
whose wit lit the literary and social scene,
she lets no standards slip; her style her defence
against invasion, deafness, her six decades.
'I write. From smoke and silence that much remains.'

Her diary lists a litany of names:
lovers, friends, musicians, poets – lost;
black holes within the galaxy of fame.
Her random notes compose their requiem,
expose the pain of war, protest its waste

as Warsaw is smashed to smouldering smithereens.

She edits, dressmaker-like, her latest manuscript,
reshaping cut strips, lips pursed with pins.
Horn-rimmed spectacles enlarging eyes young men
still praise, shoes white with ash, she is the first
to enter grotesque chambers, disclose the fate
designed, she wrote, by human minds for human kind.
From that crucible of crime, she creates
exquisite cameos, Poland's war-time masterpiece.

Her journal reveals what effort accompanies
the charm and intellect the public sees.
Women note her modish maquillage,
repeat rumours of a lover – 'Imagine, at her age!'
Feted in London, Paris, Moscow, Prague,
in as many languages she holds centre stage,
'Young sir, my powder compact, please, it's on the chair,
and yes, if you would, my silver fur...'

A laureate lady with a scalpel pen, large and generous,
her gift is to make others feel great and glamorous,
while with ruthless precision she prises life apart
and probes the subtle workings of the human heart

St. James, Ochota - Karen Kovacik

The frescoes are burning, in sunlight and in gloom,
at Sunday Mass, or with a single widow praying,
because they were painted with a tindery hand,
because the fingers that held the brush knew pleasure,
knew where to touch, for how long, with what pressure,
and there was no need to call the beloved "beloved"
because she saw the rich arterial reds of her body,
the umber of brow and belly, transmuted
in the suffering of saints. Didn't she pose
as Joan? Didn't she writhe against a drape of purple,
didn't the blaze scorch her calves, her thighs,
hot on the bowl of her hips, her unchaste breasts?
And when the flames touched her throat,
there was no color for her keening, so the painter chose
restraint, elongation, the ecstatic silence
of Peter hanging naked on an inverted cross
or Paul suffering lightning bolts to the eyes.
This painter was no stranger to illumination,
to doves big as owls descending, to virgins
gazing at angels armed with swords of love.
He had seen the capital desolate, all habitation
forsaken, loose horses wandering the avenues
as in a wilderness. This painter had smelled dynamite
and hid in sewers, discovered a talent for small acts
of sabotage, and once rescued a stranger's piano.
Later, there was nothing to do but mix bloody colours
in the unaccustomed calm. Later, there was no need
to paint devils because eleven fresh apostles
had risen from the palette of hell. These frescoes are burning,
and I'm listening to their silence:
speak, you flame-tongued supplicants and martyrs,
O speak, evangelists of shrapnel and of wax.

An Inconspicuous Man - Marek Kochan

"Well, I'm getting old but I'll tell you about your Granddad. How did he swim out to sea? Well, he swam and swam and then he stopped swimming. And the devil knows what happened then. These masks on the wall - who knows where they're from. He collected so many different things, from Africa, China, Borneo. He swam everywhere. And who sailed with him? Well, the captain, of course, he was the captain's cook. Every ship must have one. Noodles, for example. And more. For the entire crew. And then he'd wash the dishes. And what did he do, then, after he'd swum abroad? The same. Continued being a cook, only in town. Worked in a restaurant, and afterwards in the canteen of some institution or other. Did the cooking and after the meal was finished, washed the dishes.

Mind you, your grandfather was no ordinary cook, but a hero. Scared of no one. True, he was stumpy, but cunning into the bargain, and really brave. Do you think the sea frightened him? And when he stopped swimming, he was afraid of no one.

Once he was in an incident, you know. You should know your Granddad was really hard-working. He'd often take on extra work to earn more money. After all, there were seven mouths to feed. After work he'd help out at weddings. Come back late, tired, lugging heavy bags with kitchen utensils in them and various tasty things to eat, fruit, cured meat and the like. One day … actually night it was, he came back from some wedding or party, from work, I mean. The street and the courtyard were desolate, windows dark, dead silent. Granddad was carrying his plastic bags and put them on the ground, rummaged in his pockets, found his key to the staircase, took it out, opened, held the door with his shoe, came inside. The bags were heavy and large, barely fitted through the doorway, it was dark.

Suddenly someone jumped out at him saying "Hand over me your money!" and waving some instrument or other; you couldn't tell if it was a knife, a bat, or a gun. Granddad was small, the thug was enormous. Granddad was calm, tired, while the other one leapt out of the darkness shouting: "Give me the money!" What should he do? Granddad put the bags on the floor and started looking for something. "Faster, faster," said the other one. Granddad, bent down, looking for something, rummaging in his bags. Suddenly he took out a huge knife used for cutting meat, almost a chopper. So huge, so wide, a fat kitchen cleaver, which would be good for flaying pigs and cutting bones. And Granddad approached the thug with the knife, put it near his nose, said,

76

"Come on, then! Have at me, you cur!" Well, the thug was totally confused, raised his hands in the air, and didn't know what he should do. "Give me the money, now," said Granddad. The other one started shaking, fearing he might get a beating with this huge chopper, his head would come off sure as anything. He did not know what it was all about. Whom had he come across? The thug had expected a shy, inconspicuous person but your Granddad jumped out with such a murderous cleaver. Maybe he was a cannibal carrying a quartered corpse in his bags? The mugger was shaking all over, so he promptly took out some small change not knowing what to do with it. "Down On the ground!" said your Granddad. The other one threw money, while Granddad told him, "Get lost!". The other guy rushed to the door, yanked the handle, fled to the courtyard and only his shoes slapped as he ran until he disappeared in the darkness. Fearful as God knows what, happy to have escaped with his life. And Granddad packed his tools of the trade, took the bags and went to the lift. He opened the flat as quietly as possible, because everyone was asleep. He went to bed.

And the money? Well, he picked up the money in the morning. It was not much, a couple of zlotys. Apparently the other one had not yet lined his pockets that night. My Granddad took what was there, went to buy cigarettes – it was enough for two packets of Zefir.

And the thug? No-one knows. He was scared, that's for sure. Maybe he even gave up his criminal ways, afraid he would not go unharmed for the second time. There were never such incidents again at our place. Your Granddad was like that. A true hero, but a quiet and an inconspicuous man."

Translated by Katarzyna Waldegrave

The Palace of Babel - Wojciech Maślarz

"Mine eyes have seen the building of the Palace of Babel"
said Honzik, a drunk from Jelinku but a kind of prophet;
I'm sure he was referring to the Warsaw one that Stalin
called his 'Gift to Polish People,' monstrosity of kitsch
that "Culture and Science" cats, rats, and businesses inhabit,
once on a human Chmielna Street the Germans bombed to bits,
now its huge statue, gazing like a sphinx, of our Adam Mickiewicz
while Honzik, with his beetroot face, too scarlet to be Communist:
-- no party-climbing hack was he, just one of the gabbling rabble -
"And mine ears have heard the multi-lingual incoherent babble" -
he meant perhaps the newspeak cant that politicians parled in.
Now glass towers shrink the monumental kink, and Mammon
in Golden Terraces of Empik and Arcadia kicks old Socialism - its
Utopia has gone. When clean consumers sip non-alcoholic fizz,
strong Vodka let Honzik see the Palace then for what it really is.

Bar Schwejk Beggary - Andrew Fincham

Across the fence
Which marks
Café Society
From the street

I passed the drunk
Three coins
To buy a beer

Knowing I
(But for the grace of God)
Drink there.

Millennium Drift - Jacek Podsiadło

When death comes, you have to be in the spot it comes to, otherwise it's all for naught

To Dorota Różycka

With the New Year I resolved to start a new life.

No more delays.

No more iniquities.

No more Martinis on the express train to Krakow, when the boredom of the journey is ameliorated by the fine reading of fine literature while one is slightly and elegantly inebriated.
No more reading, that's the most important thing.
I sat down to write one last farewell poem called "Fantasy."

Fantasy
To Fantasia
I fantasized that one day again…

I didn't finish the rest of it because I couldn't figure out anything that rhymed with "again" besides "a fen," to which I took an immediate disliking.
I fantasized that one day again, we would roll into a fen, …?

Fantasia and I had never really done much rolling in fens.I soaked the paper I had prepared for my one last farewell poem in water and used the resulting gloop to seal up the window.
Which is how "Papier-mâché II" came about.
I took the gum out of my mouth and used it to cover up the peep hole in the door.

I covered up all the ventilation egresses in the kitchen and the bathroom with the first pictures to hand.
This reminded me of when Letycja, who was still really little at the time, on seeing her two grandmothers at once had said, "Horrible old egresses."
Outside you could hear the first champagne corks and fireworks. I turned off the lights.
I turned on all the gas taps, lay down on the kitchen table, and put a dog chain round my hands, because I didn't have any rosary beads. But I did have a dog, a blind dog named Fantasia.

No more blind dogs.
The hiss of the burners diminished, blending pleasantly with the echoes of shots and cheers coming in from everywhere.
When the gunfire and screams reached their apogee, something strange happened.

The hiss stopped altogether.
I cleared my throat. Pensively, I rubbed my chin. I got up, turned on the light, and reached for the Christmas edition of the paper.
In the box with emergency phone numbers I found the number for the gas company. Despite the dog chain on my hands, I managed to dial it.
"Is this the gas emergency service?"
"Gas it is."
"Happy New Year."
"Gas men always at the ready."
"I thank God for that. And I actually just lost my gas, Mr Gasman."
"When?"
"Just now, right at midnight, I think."
"Yeah, we were expecting that."
"What do you mean?"
"The millennium problem."
"The what problem?"
"The millennium.An omen of the end. Do you have a computer?"
"No, I write on a typewriter."
"So go to your typewriter and try to write something.Sorry, the other phone is ringing.Happy New Year."
I went to my typewriter and tried to write, Life, and Specifically the Death of Angelica de Sancé.My typewriter wasn't writing—instead of staying on the paper, the letters flew off into the air like a swarm of liberated, feminist flies.

I put on a CD by Marcel Ponseele, belting out sonatas on the oboe and bazooka, and instead d of him I got Robert Wyatt singing "Yolanda" over and over.

I couldn't figure out any way to get the CD to stop. From then on things seemed to snowball, as they say, out of control.
There were snowdrops growing in the refrigerator.

The shower kept cutting out on account of phone calls from friends asking how I was feeling this year. The vacuum cleaner threw up all its trash and decided to make babies with the hair dryer. When you flushed the toilet, the water went up and into some pipes going into the ceiling. History books on the third millennium will end with the words: "and they pissed into the reservoir."

My blind dog Fantasia, whom I fetched from the pound a few days later, had got her vision back. Now she could even see the future. She would sit there and read and read about our bizarre era in the history books. The skiers in the Four Jumps Tournament jumped backwards. A disconcerted neighbour complained to me on the steps that his wife, who always had been a good woman before, and opposed to degeneracy, now wanted to be taken from behind, and only from behind.

"That's the world gone topsy-turvy," I said, "I was reading about it in some book.
My shower cut out."
"Who cares about the shower, when your own wife only wants to be taken from behind?"
"Then take her from behind," I shrugged.
"What if I can't get a hard-on?"
"Say it as it is. I'm planning on dedicating a documentary story to these extraordinary days, for future generations, as a warning."
"But how, 'I can't get an erection,' like that?"
"Maybe you just drank too much, for New Year's Eve and everything?"

"No. I just got back from the sex doctor in Warsaw. The problem I have is a millennium problem, that's what he said. Are you doing okay with those kinds of things?"

All because of those zeros that suddenly started ending the dates. After every thought and every action there now stands a puffed-up, unavoidable zero. Shoes whose soles have snow melting on them leave a new zero on the floor at every step. A zero takes up the whole bed when I want to go to sleep, an elongated zero looks out at me in the mornings from the mirror while I shave. I have trouble getting to sleep, and I don't feel like shaving, honestly I'm shaving in spite of myself. I'm trying to read the future in the new eyes of my old dog, round like two zeros.

Translated by Jennifer Croft

The Men from Praga - Anne Berkeley

Because my Polish doesn't run to 'tram ticket',
I have to walk. And my camera's jammed.
I jab it with my gloves. Brush at orange grit
the wind flings off the tarmac. It's miles.
And anyway, the light's gone

Over the bridge, across the Vistula, is Praga
The Bear-pit, the badlands, the concrete tower blocks.
The sky weighs down on the river, beats it flat,
squeezing out the scum that snags on reeds.
I imagine heavy industries upstream.

But it isn't scum. Ice. Its invisible edge. Because,
down on the river, far from the shore:
two men crouch on camp-stools, hauling
something in from the tricky gleam, doing
delicate, intricate things with their bare hands.

I watch them. They're quite at home
out there in the channel. Smoking, fixing bait.
The winds flicks Polish at me. It's all beyond me
Their Sunday morning ease, their ice,
the fluent fish at large below their feet.

Esprit d'escalier - Stefan Golston

It was a gorgeous summer day, a school vacation time, when I was taking a walk in Saxon Park. I passed two young girls, sitting on the bench and having a lively conversation. One of them, a strong brunette, with beautiful black, slightly slanted eyes, and rosy cheeks, was holding a large red poppy on a long stem.

I was trying to be cute: "Is this flower for me?" I asked, slowing down my pace a little. Her answer was cold: "It is not."

Half an hour later, when I was returning, they still were where I left them. However she must have seen me coming, since when I approached them, she handed me a naked stem, without petals and said with mischief in her eyes: "This is for you."

That could have been all that was to it, except that several years later I married her.

Eastertide - Leo Yankevich

Gliwice

A sudden brightness. Call it day.
Rooks above the cathedral, and clouds
a thousand shades of morning grey,
while underneath: the coiling crowds
bear their pastries and precious fruit.
The cobble-stones shimmer in the rain
as 'glory, glory' the bells bruit
past the sinners along the lane.

Mother over the loaf of bread - Paweł Kubiak

A memory
in me sprawls,
a moment
in me feeds:
On the warm heater
a cat purrs, on the table
milk loaves
like true bread
as mother draws the knife blade
through the velvet of the flour
marks the sign of the cross
and we can eat.

Translated by A Fincham

Feast of Corpus Christi - Carole Satyamurti

The line snail-ribbons
Down Krakowskie Street – women,
Girls, some medalled veterans.
Slow hymns, as for a funeral;
crowds press, voices join in,
a helicopter tacking overhead.

The procession swerves,
passes the crucifix of flowers
made secretly one night, by women:
flowers as witness,
candles for endurance,
lumps of coal for solidarity.

Candles in jars, steady in the draught,
soldiers with Modigliani faces.
It is their grandmothers
who bring fresh flowers each day,
work them in calmly, eyes lowered
as their knees roughen on stone?

It could be their sisters,
surge of first-communion white,
who know the hymns by heart,
who bear these banners
embroided with an image from the East:
a Madonna, black as coal.

The Big Match - Andrew Fincham

Sometimes you can be sitting in a bar so long you start to feel you might be doing something useful. I mean to say, you might have something useful to do if you stay in the bar a little longer. Some people think that if you can stay in that long you can have nothing to do, but what do they know? I remember lots of times when people left the bar, and then something happened. It happens all the time.

My grandfather used to say the secret is liking what you do, not doing what you like. If he'd not spent so little time in bars, he would have known you can do both. It's really quite easy. The last place you have to do things that you don't like, or not do things you do like, is in a bar.

That's why people go there.

That's why you'll find me there. Or here, for that matter.

I came in because there was a big match. It happens a lot.

Somebody, somewhere, sets up a big match with one set of people against another set, and before you know where you are you're here because there's a big match on the big screen in the big bar. I prefer the small bar – it's smaller, and everyone knows everyone, unless they don't go in there. I come in for the big matches most of the time. I wasn't sure which one it was this time, but then again they're mostly the same.

And it's sometimes important to be seen, if you know what I mean. The place to be seen can be bigger than the size of the screen. Here it is so important that they don't even need one, just a television on a wheeled stand, rather like they used to bring in at school. I wasn't terribly attentive at school. Didn't really do much at Oxford, either, come to that. I roomed with a chap who went in for the law. We used to play cards for cocktails – the most horrible combinations were placed in a glass and the loser drank it down. Never knew the man to protest at the prescription. He was a gentleman. When we ran out of cocktails we'd play games with matches, or would duel with flaming matches from opposite armchairs. Never knew him to flinch, not even when his pubescent chest hair began to smoulder on his pubescent chest.
His own fault for wearing an open necked shirt – a tie would have prevented the problem. And burned hair does smell so.

This is a very good place to be seen. The Pink Elephant Club, of the British Embassy, in Warsaw, Poland. The Pink Club. There's a pink elephant on the wall by the window, which helps to remind people where they are, and they're a pleasant set of chaps, by and large. Particularly during a big match. They have free matches here. That's one reason why I've been here for so long. Been coming here, for the matches. They used to have free matches in a brick on the bar – unless that was somewhere else – but either way, the nice thing is, if you like that sort of thing - you can't buy a drink at the bar. Not in the least.

Now, for some, that may be a disadvantage but it suits me. People get shirty, trying to buy a drink during a big match, but they say the same to everybody. No drinks for sale. But there are drinks, of course there are – it's a bar, and there's a big match. The secret is – and I don't think I'm dropping any bricks here, but keep it under your hat – you buy a little blue ticket. They sell little blue tickets, and you exchange them for a drink. It's childishly simple. A child could do it. But not in here, obviously, that would be against the rules. The best tickets have more than one drink on them, and when people buy them, each time they take a drink one of the chaps behind the bar crosses off a little box, to show that the chap has had the drink. Quite often, when they leave, some of the little boxes are not crossed off, and they just leave them on the bar. Or on the floor, that sort of thing. They're still alive. That's another good reason why this is a good place. Not in the small bar, of course. We're rather more careful. And we look after the living, so to speak.

So I was here today for the big match. It happened this afternoon, they tell me, and we lost. There were Australians who beat us, someone said, so I suppose it was a cricket match. Or a rugby. I couldn't swear to the score, but I believe there was a ten in it. I had a bit of luck earlier on. There was a blue ticket with a good number of little boxes uncrossed when the man left it, and in quite a bad mood. He should have stayed.

Something has happened.

An Australian boy has been moving along the bar, performing some trick for money. Some kind of tourist, with his hair and a large red mackintosh. He's been betting people for money. Not something I'd do. Not that I'm short, I'm over five and a half foot, but the rent is due tomorrow and a chap passed over the necessary to help me out of a short difficulty. Now the boy has just finished with the last fellow, and he's heading over to me. He wants to bet the contents of his pocket book against mine. He's got his out, and is waving

it about the small bar. Everyone is looking, expecting me to follow suit, I've no doubt.
Certainly not. I've no interest in his schemes. Anyway, the money is spoken for. Five thousand zloty.
From what they say, he claims I cannot take a match from a box and light it using only one hand. In a quarter of a minute. I wonder just how hard can that be?

*

He seemed very disappointed. He claimed I'd cheated, and that I'd done it before. They had to throw him out. Without his wallet, of course.

I was slightly disappointed myself. My college best was under ten seconds.

Does anyone have a Bluey? In The Pink.

The cry of nie ma - James G. Coon

drobne?
drobne?

nie ma!
nie ma!

there is never
any small change.

the kiosks, the skleps,
the department stores,
everywhere
we have no small change.

someone finally
explained why:

Poland has
been short-changed
by history, he said.

that's the
best explanation
I ever heard.

Cupid in Praga - Grażyna Tatarska

In Warsaw's Praga, May's run riot with the scent of lilac.
Long-legged girls soar in the colours of the morning...

You sit glumly at the bus stop – the bus wheels squirt mud.
You get up, wave your fists and then you see her...

You chase the overcrowded bus with Cupid's arrow.
Sinful thoughts hone in on the girl's legs.

Let speech recover words, the poem retrieve its message.

Someone has darted off in frills, in ribbons, into this May...
in a muddy bus in Grochowska Street in the morning.

Translated by Stefan Bodlewski

My Polish Widower - Karen Kovacik

The cliché about your life passing before your eyes at the moment of death, I discovered, is only partially true. I had just sped across four lanes of traffic on Warsaw's notorious Wislostrada, when a beer truck cut me off. One minute I was braking hard behind a four-foot bottle of Okocim Porter, rumored to be the late Pope's favorite brew, and the next I was sailing through the windshield of my husband's tiny Daewoo. I had time for only a few scenes from my life – autobiographical greatest hits - before I found myself in the proverbial tunnel of light.

Oddly, one of those scenes was Driver's Ed in Hammond, Indiana, taught by Mr. Krebs, the eternally patient woodshop teacher, as if death by car crash had rendered null and void my hard-earned C in the subject decades before. Had I been driving that '75 Monte Carlo instead of Tomek's fiberglass breadbox, I might well have survived. Instead, I began acquainting myself with the rights and privileges of the newly deceased. I could now spy on my husband any time I wanted.

My first glimpse of heaven's gate reminded me of Warsaw itself, specifically the Central Train Station, with its fluorescent lighting, platforms of waiting passengers, and staticky loud-speakers announcing arrivals and departures. The officiating angel, who resembled an auto mechanic in his glowing striped jumpsuit, explained that while the omnipresence would kick in immediately, omniscience would be granted more gradually. 'Trust me,' he said. 'Sometimes it's better not to know.'

I always hoped that if I preceded Tomek in death, I'd be admitted into the labyrinth of his mind. You can perceive a lot about a spouse – his appetite for jellied carp or fondness for solitary reading or devotion to friends - and still be awed by the extent to which he remains unknown. Add to the mix our linguistic and cultural differences and the fact that Tomek had spent considerable time alone before he met me. Solitude made him a watcher, not a talker. Had it not been for my garrulous, semi-coherent Polish, which propelled him to fits of extroversion, we would never have fallen in love. The fact is that husbands and wives never love each other equally. And in my marriage to Tomek, I was the one who loved more. I with my lisping American accent, big soft ass, and dyed blonde hair that frizzed in the rain. Ever since I made him smile during our first English lesson some 13 years ago, he had been my elegant boulevard, and I his tornado.

For that first meeting, we had agreed on Warsaw's Constitution Square, a post-Communist hybrid of massive limestone steelworkers and the neon logos of a global marketplace. The Café Hortex located there was itself a throwback to the former centralized economy, each miniature bistro table topped by a cheap porcelain sugar bowl and a drinking glass filled with a cone of worthless tissue napkins. While waiting for Tomek to arrive, I stared at my wedge of strawberry gelatin cake, attempting with all my power to resist it. Impatient waitresses swished past in their apple-green uniforms, and some grandpa at the next table hummed along with the radio. I had ample time to review the grammar and vocabulary lesson I'd prepared. I was dressed in the wool skirt and high-necked cotton blouse that I always wore for first lessons because they minimized my ridiculous curves. My tall black boots remained home in the closet, and on my feet were flats so sensible I felt embarrassed to wear them in public. On the phone Tomek had told me he was an architect, 33 years old, and gave his height in centimeters, which led me to expect a fairly tall man. In person, however, he was no more than five feet, in a blue raincoat and corduroys, with one of those small Polish shoulder bags, a kind of purse for men. I must have outweighed him by twenty pounds. That day's lesson was to be on verbs of motion - a refresher since Tomek had already studied English for five years. I poured him some jasmine tea from my pot, slopping a little onto his purse in the process, and started talking about coming and going. Maybe it was the radio's Chopin sonata unspooling its vehement silk or Tomek's blue-eyed amusement at my careful lesson, but

I suddenly knew we would be good in bed together. 'To come has another meaning in English,' I found myself explaining, then offered examples: 'She was never able to come with him' and 'He made me come five times in one night.' That's when Tomek smiled. Tomek was in the tea aisle at the Hala Kopiska when the call came from the city police. He'd just bypassed all the fruity herbals, the wild strawberry and blueberry I loved, in favor of the dense black grains that inspired him to flights of architectural fancy. I watched Tomek flip open the tiny mobilnik and answer with his typical subdued 'Tak, slucham.' He stiffened when the policeman identified himself, a predictable reaction among Poles of Tomek's age. Then a look of wonder crossed his face, the same perplexed curiosity he exhibited when I mixed up two unrelated but similar-sounding Polish nouns. 'Yes, Carla's American. 44 years old.' He didn't cry or make a scene, but looked so pale and shaky that security didn't stop him when he walked off with a tin of premier Darjeeling. The sight of my petite Tomek straining against the November wind made me wish I had proceeded with greater caution into those four lanes of Wislostrada traffic. I longed to wrap his muffler around his neck – one of those motherly gestures he despised.

It was only in the elevator to our ninth-floor flat - the narrow, mirror adorned lift where we hauled up groceries and argued about French cinema and once almost made love - that my Polish husband, now my widower, permitted himself a couple of tears. I had seen him cry on two occasions in our marriage: the death of his favorite aunt and the time I drank one Wyborowa too many on New Year's Eve and French-kissed a lecherous poet in the buffet line. Of course, Tomek was not one to sniffle at a party. He drove us home in silence, forcing me to endure the avalanche of his disapproval and hurt, and averted his eyes during the interminable elevator ride. It was only in the bedroom, after I stripped off my low-backed jade dress and attempted to convert everything I couldn't say into a no-holds-barred seduction that I was stunned to see him cry. A reddening of the nose, a quick shame-struck covering of the eyes. We were in bed, he seated with his back to the wall, and when I noticed his tears, I pulled him on top of me in a fierce American hug. I called him by name, I called him beloved, I stroked his hair and neck and back and butt and hissed in his ear, 'I want to make love to show you how sorry I am.' He arched up on his elbows as if taking my measure. In his coldest, most official-sounding Polish, he said 'You're not capable of that.'

'Let me show you.' I knew that mind games always aroused him. His blue-gray eyes were already dry and alert. 'Nie.' The monosyllable of refusal resounded with arctic finality, though his penis seemed of a different persuasion. In the end, Tomek let me know the terms my apology would have to take: he would thrust me very slowly sixty times. With each stroke, I was to tell him I was sorry for kissing that horny idiot, Waldemar. I was not to have an orgasm until or after this sixtieth stroke despite the fact that he knew very well - we had been married three years – how to bring me to the brink. The legalistic precision of his terms amused me, nudged me from abject to ironic. Mercy fresh from the freezer was better than no mercy at all.

'Jak chcesz' I said. 'As you wish.'

And so it began, so we began, the first ten superficial as a blueprint, my faint 'I'm sorrys' rote with defiance. Around twenty, I started to feel the architec-tonics of him, the subtle buttressing of his pride, his fear of losing me. At thirty five, I began to cry myself, so I could scarcely whisper the thick phrase of apology: przepraszam. Thirty eight, thirty nine, random images of my love for him: the care he took when defrosting our tiny fridge, tilting it back on an orthographic dictionary, or our evening walks through the Park of Happiness, the willows and poplars cascading toward the ground. Forty five, forty six, his nuanced finger on my clitoris; fifty, fifty two, the choir loft

93

shrieking with sopranos; fifty three, his blue eyes dark with lust; fifty seven, the counterpoint of our breathing; fifty eight, fighting the aria inside me, and finally Sixty; Sixty, Sixty.

In the tiny, mustard-tiled kitchen, Tomek plugged in the electric kettle, pried open the tea tin with a spoon, and covered the bottom of a glass with dense black leaves. The kitchen looked much as I had left it. The same windowpane dishtowel hung on its hook, and a heel of rye rested on the table, cut side down. How odd to spy on one's own life, one's own husband. I felt like a member of the secret police, a tajnik, watching him this way, for my Polish husband valued privacy above everything. Tomek called one of his friends, an artist with a century-old apartment in the Mokotów district, to cancel their afternoon meeting. They were supposed to have been planning the new kolorystyka of the flat – a bolder look with ultramarine cushions and citron-colored walls. I didn't need even limited omniscience to predict that the artist, Grzegorz P., would invite Tomek over for a drink, would even pick him up since my widower, thanks to me, no longer had a car. Nor was I surprised when Tomek, surrounded by my headbands, hats, and scarves, confronted by my breakfast dishes in the drainer, accepted the invitation with gratitude.

My husband had always liked working with artists because they had feasible intuitions, and typically they bartered a painting for a design.

He dreaded the dithery clients who had no sense they were ruining a teak Saarinen coffee table by cluttering it with a souvenir ashtray, week-old newspapers, and TV remote. I approached that category myself with my fondness for kiosk kitsch such as the little felt rooster that I used to display on the moderne étagère until Tomek could bear it no longer and threw it in our building's incinerator. It happened that Grzegorz grew up in the southern mountain resort town of Zakopane, the only place in Poland where cognac was the primary drink instead of vodka or beer. So in Grzegorz's high-ceilinged flat, adorned with elaborate sconces shaped like lilies, the brandy snifters appeared immediately, along with a bottle of some high-octane Armagnac. Had I not been dead, I would have enjoyed handling one of those glassy bells, twirling the rich brown liquor within, and taking its plummy wood-smoke into my mouth. Which is what my widower was doing, seated in the straight-backed chair that his host had provided for him so he wouldn't disappear into the sofa. Grzegorz, too, was cradling a swollen snifter, his long legs in blue jeans stretched beneath the table, the beginnings of a belly spilling over his belt.

In their circle of friends Grzegorz threw the best parties and had the most women. And while he typically favored Art Academy brunettes – if the young things hanging on him at gallery openings were any indication – I more than once caught him staring at my ass. He had a surveyor's gaze, an instinct for declivity and rise. Regardless of how intelligently I managed to talk about twentieth-century painting, including his own geometrized portraits, I was always aware of that narrowing of the eyes, that sense of appraisal. With Tomek, Grzegorz displayed none of that judicious weighing. It pleased me to watch how skillfully he manoeuvred the conversation to put my widower at ease, starting out with recent Warsaw buildings. And Tomek, though he never swore in my

presence because of some old-fashioned notion of courtliness, used even the most notorious Polish words for describing Roman Z.'s green monstrosity of a supermarket. Eventually, however, Grzegorz brought up the subject of my abrupt demise.

"Co zrobisz teraz bez Carli?" No American would ever ask a bereaved friend straight out how he'd manage now that his wife was gone, but the question seemed unremarkable to Tomek. "God knows." Tomek swirled the brandy around in his glass.

"Even though a dozen times she almost drove me to divorce."

Were I not dead, I would have grabbed that beautiful glass from his hand and flung the drink in his lap. Sure we fought, operatically even, Tomek locking himself in his room, and I swearing at him through the door in English. He was the sort of person who would measure an entire wall before hanging a single picture on it, while I would use every dish in the kitchen when preparing a three-course meal. The Polish equivalents of "Quiet down" and "Get a grip on yourself" were Tomek's favorite and absolutely enraging rejoinders to me.

"While I myself don't believe in marriage," Grzegorz said, "I must say you and she seemed content enough."

I recognized that appraising gleam. Grzegorz wanted to find out something about me, something he never dared ask while I was alive, I could feel it. "It's just that Carla was, in many ways, a child," Tomek said. "You know what Americans are like. They're served the wrong dish at a restaurant, and it's cause for war." He sipped his drink for dramatic emphasis. "On the other hand, they can't wait to see what the Christmas Angel will bring." Grzegorz laughed at this ridiculous national stereotype which I allegedly fit. For the record, I have to say that during our entire marriage, I threw precisely one tantrum at the Restauracja Staropolska, when the waiter not only brought me a dried out schnitzel instead of the Kotlet de Volaille, but also dribbled gravy on my purple wool suit. And as for the Christmas Angel, the Polish counterpart of Santa Claus, I admit I did look forward to my annual gift, but that's only because Tomek chose so well. A red silk peignoir one year, a book of idioms the next. Grzegorz assumed that insinuating posture once again.

"But certainly, Carla jako kobieta loved you very much." The phrase "as a woman" dripped with innuendo.

Tomek, slouching in his chair, looked bereft. I had always wondered if the dead found comfort in the grief of the living. The answer in my case was clearly yes. Without looking up, my widower muttered,

"I never knew a woman who liked it so much."

Grzegorz seized his chance. "I suppose she wanted it all the time."
Tomek nodded. "In the car, or at the movies. Even at the Filharmonia once during intermission."

My widower always sweated when drunk, and he was sweating now, poor thing, a hand clamped over his eyes. His voice didn't rise above a mumble. "She was wearing that ginger perfume I loved," he said, "and some huge vulgar pearls, obviously fake. We'd gone to hear Schubert and Schumann, and by the break, Carla was so pent up she couldn't sit still." Truth is, I moaned so extravagantly in Tomek's ear that he draped his coat over our laps and slid an expert hand up my velvet skirt. It was like whole notes followed by thirty-second notes. More scherzo than lieder.

"We pretend to miss the soul or the mind," Grzegorz said, softer now.

"When it's the body we can't live without."

My widower stared into his empty glass as if to confirm the truth of this remark. I thought how every night I enfolded his slender back into me, blanketing him with my scent and softness and warmth. We'd fall asleep with my nose in his hair, my hands tight around his waist. His tongue often tasted like tea. The prospect of never sleeping with him again seemed unbearable. Was this how haunting began? While playing with one of the sconces in Grzegorz's flat, I managed to ring the bell at the reception desk in heaven. Behind the desk a window opened onto a frenetic scene. The newly arrived, pale and travel-worn, carried twine-bound parcels and dented valises up interminable escalators. But a pitcher of lilies rested on the desk itself, as did an enormous box of chocolates. That grease monkey of an angel in his glowing, striped jumpsuit was chewing on a cloud-colored pen.

"Yeah?" he said.
"Sorry," I told him, "but I'm not cut out for this place."
"Says who?"
"Me" I said. "I miss living too much. Heretical as this might sound, I'd give it all up, even the eternal bliss, for one more night of bed with Tomek."
"Hold on, you're getting ahead of yourself." The angel looked at his fat silver donut of a watch, marked with an infinity of years instead of hours. "You'll be having relations again with your husband in 31.5 years."

Without asking for permission, I helped myself to a truffle filled with persimmon and spice.
"You've got to be kidding. I want him now."
"Tough. Your old man's not due to give up the ghost till he's 75."
"How will he die?" I figured I might as well use the angel's ESP to my advantage.
"Cancer of the liver. Awful way to go, but his wife will be by his side the whole time."
"His what?"
"Lady, you heard me. Can't expect the guy to live like a priest for thirty years."

I didn't feel like being schooled in sexual mores by an angel. Jealousy hit me worse than a thousand windshields. I grabbed another chocolate, this one flavored with violets and champagne. How could Tomek marry again?

"So who's the lucky bride?" I sneered.
"Girl named Beata S., twenty years his junior. They'll meet next year at the opening of her sculpture show." He gazed again into the crystal ball of his wristwatch. "And they'll marry three months later."

I pictured one of Grzegorz's Art Academy brunettes wearing only a bridal veil, straddling Tomek on our narrow bed. To comfort myself, I imagined that she had flunked out of French and had only minimal English, though of course she'd prattle on in Polish with a native's flair.

"Will they be happy together?"

The angel shrugged. "What marriage is completely happy? Tomek will be lonely without you. He'll be impressed with Beata's sculptures, which in my opinion are a little weird, though the Holy Spirit likes them—they're these huge black and purple gourds wrapped in fabric. She'll chat with him, make him feel appreciated, and to be honest, she's not unattractive." The angel paused to see how I'd absorbed his prophecy. I rolled my eyes.

"But soon enough," he continued, "she'll consider him an old man. Someone to be coddled and sheltered from the truth. She'll take other lovers, and Tomek will again miss you and your passion."

Hearing about my widower in this way, I felt like an audience member in some upper balcony at an opera. The story reached me from such a distance it inspired only pity and not a lightning of the soul. So now Tomek would be the one to love more.

I glared at the angel. "So I'm supposed to park myself on a cloud till he gets ready to die?"

"Truth is," he said, "you're slated for purgatory." I wasn't eligible for heaven, the angel informed me, because in life I had neglected to cultivate patience. In purgatory, I'd be obliged to wait and then wait some more. They'd assign me a narrow cell with five ticking clocks all set for eternity. I would pray rosaries, endless white beads slipping through my fingers, and meditate till my mind stilled. Regular field trips to earth would be manda-tory. I'd have to watch as Tomek brewed countless pots of tea, walked alone in the Park of Happiness, and made love with Beata S.

"You'll learn," said the angel, "that you can get through desire without giving in to it." He looked me straight in the eye to drive his point home, his voice both stern and kind.

I reached once more into the box of chocolates. My hand closed over what looked like a petit-four adorned with a buttercup. But this time I glanced at the angel for permission. When he nodded assent, I popped the confec-tion in my mouth and let it dissolve slowly. It was a chocolate of final things, more bitter than espresso, dashed with the salt of regret, and dense as the densest loam of the earth.

Courtyard: woman with rosary - Jennifer Robertson

Women sit contentedly in the kindly sun.
This is their final home.
A many-windowed building of honeyed stone
bounds a secluded yard,
an erstwhile convent, cut off from town.
That busy world is no longer even a distant hum.
The place is graced by a name: Caritas.
The women are the recipients, saggy bundles
in motley hand-me-downs.
No one has much now to call her own.
The charity is in the peace
of gnarled hands at rest on faded dress.
There is anchorage and quiet haven here, giving space
for small things: sulks and pettiness;
and smiles and well-worn reminiscence.
One woman sits apart.
Her sleek brown head does not belong,
it seems, to the general throng.
She clutches warm, black beads.
The moorings of her memory have gone
and the rhythms of the rosary, like a childhood song
comfort her as she drifts, placidly, along.
Sometimes foreigners encroach upon her enclosed space,
strange beings from some fabled place;
and then she is most anxious to please.
'Anglais? Francais?" she enquires, and serenades
her visitors with 'La Marseilleise'.
And now we see a book-lined salon,
glasses of golden tea, and a young girl brought in
to charm her mother's guests
with songs she has learnt from her French governess.
The melodies still sing, though words are lost.

Fred Recalls - Ella Risbridger

He saw the Tsar's army.

War games filled the lives of the children in this town. It was 1914, and the army of the Russian Tsar was marching through on their way to fight the Germans. But the children didn't care. They fought imaginary wars with teams of children, girls as nurses who ran away at the sight of blood, boys who were soldiers with wooden weapons. The older ones, commanding their platoon, sent out messengers in the shape of small boys, riebionek, who were presented with toffees, humbugs, sweets of many kinds and calibres. Later, when the children's war games had progressed, the boys were sent by the older leaders to steal munitions from the Russians, no Russian soldier suspecting that the young boy who collected sweets was stealing bullets behind their backs. From these bullets they made their own bombs, with gunpowder and the fragmented remains of the bullet casing, throwing them into water and eagerly awaiting the "fwoosh!"

A real soldier at last! First the compulsory join-up letter, then the medical check, then the training, and now.... a real soldier, armed with real weapons, not wooden planks and broken fence-posts, as he had played with as a child. His many missions, too numerous to count or even remember most of them, sabotaging and escaping in cramped claustrophobia, running, hiding and always on the run.

*

The old man sits with his wife and his friends. "Ninety-four next birthday!" he says. Sharing beers and apple pastries, sharing his stories of the days he has seen. They want to honour him now, decorate him with the medals he has lost. "We'll see," he says to those who want to know whether they can. "We'll see." An old man sitting in a café with his wife. A young boy begging sweets from the Russian soldiers. A commando leaping from planes. A saboteur destroying bridges and railways. An adolescent having supper with the last archduke's physician. One and the same.

100

Mizeria Kawalera - John a'Beckett

Yesterday the carton of milk that opens like a tin when you tear it;
the wind that slams the window shut without breaking the glass
or, if it does, your somehow being able to grin and bear it.

Yesterday the handle that remains on the door-- after you turn it;
your Polish friend's moustache that remains on his face and in tact
because your cigarette lighter's flame stuck on the right size when
you went to light the fag in his gob, didn't flare up and burn it.

Yesterday, rather than emerging at the last minute after you've
strained your last muscle up to the point where you think the bug'll
never come out and it does at last minute causing your knuckle
to hit you in the face. Yesterday the cork flows out of its groove,
smoothly out of the bottle without any pain—just like The Puggle

But Today the struggle

Tomorrow in the water that flows out of the tap, a perfect balance
of the body and mind and the hot and cold water in the shower,
not the burn-and-freeze murder. The kanapka opens--early flower
of Spring! The lids that come off all the containers you have -oh!-
and the cereal packet you don't have to stab open like the mother
of Norman Bates stabbing a detective in Alf Hitchcock's "Psycho",
The vegemite that into the country you don't have to smuggle

But Today the struggle

Today the marketing call when you're in the middle of cooking,
the letter-box filled with junk mail, the tearing the milk carton open
so the milk goes all over your face; the painting falls off the wall
in the middle of the night, not onto the floor, no, it falls onto you
because it was stuck on with the government's idea of glue.

Today the normal friendship that becomes a sour romantic blur
when your Polish girl-friend rings you up at midnight in a blue
fit, saying she'd been waiting an infernal half-hour for you
when you thought you'd been waiting half an hour for her.

Tomorrow: nothing amiss, Yesterday- bliss
In both aspects of time, a glorious absence of strife.
But with just about everything in a bachelor's life...
(Oh for a bed in which you could curl up and snuggle!)

No, Today the struggle.

Polish Autumn - Andrew Fincham

If there must be
October
let it come in like a lamb
as Spring did once begin
to welcome leaves
in green from summer's sun
& flowers
with petals still to shed
as paler shadows lengthen

A gentle end to earth's year's labour
field and garden
eased towards
a fallow winter's
quiet domain

But let October ring
such colours
that the heart can rise above
still mists
in glorious reds and orange

Singing
with the falling of the leaves
Just quite how much
is made by us
(& how much more
we owe to thee).

The Tatras - Mohamed Ben Younes

Consider me lover, murmur to me
your wisdom, mountains of the south.
Take me for Judas, raise my rebel soul
on your saddles, your council teaching me
about the North, all my wrongs,
long excuses whose verse you know;
your straddled voice ever reaching me
in a melange of muses and vertigo.

The marmot hisses in my heart
a strand of joy and its tendency
as the clement sky's
winds harry, harass, enfold and
pester me. Tender, grand territory.
So do your hearts,
do your eyes
You daughters of Poland!

White river, clear, unsullied by ravages
run through my veins like a breeze in me.
Extinguish the fire of that country bruised by
Algeria's tears and her vengeances.
Here a valley holds out its trees for me
so that I can cross by
the lily and the bodies
Soiled by weapon or lie.

Bring out the cascade in me,
you streams, let me dream in my fall
that a water out of me now washes all
my past tendencies-gone.
I'm in love with felicity
as in the Battle of Ghetto Warszawa:
that lifeless child of the Dream Memorial
reaches as if to feed the female cadaver.

Sailing to Sopot - Stephen Romer

In a brown smoky room
to the North of Central Europe
we lolled over a tablecloth

and remote waiters
lolled
against the sideboard;

outside, under cloud,
the chrome blue Baltic
sported its swans and oily fringe.

To the right
Gdansk, with its angular
unsellable gantries
and ahead, the narrow arm
of Hel peninsula
where the dog roses blow.

We never got there, and my feeble pun
to be postmarked Hel
was prevented by the military.

So we went to Sopot,
rounding the corner at Westerplatte
and sailed out of history

on a stretch of open sea
where the Grand Hotel
emerged above the glitter;

it might have been Cabourg,
or the Lido,
with Aschenbach among us

in the little ferry
filled with Polish children.
I could see him, muffled up,
in one of the ample basket chairs,

which faced in all directions
that deserted day in early March

when over a soiled tablecloth
I discoursed on time and the past
so sentimentally you grew restive

and rolled your beer green eyes,
zielono-piwne, longing to be out
in the sound of the sea

szum and morze, the words
come back to me, your mouth
was the seashell, close to my ear.

Mid Air - Joanna Szczepkowska

A man in torn but glossy boots
leans over the dustbin. In his arms
a violin and bow, but I can't know
if he takes them out or does he throw
them in? Can't pluck the courage up
to turn around and check what's so
I pass by on the other side and wait
for his street debut .Just silence till
in a moment there's a special, late
komponenta of sound: a knock
of wood, a vanishing of boots,
a sigh as they go- a fact in it
that this contemporary music
doesn't know a limit.

Translated by Karolina Maslarz

Auschwitz 25th January 2005 - Andrew Fincham

Sixty Years ago
The best and worst
Machine of death
The world has known
Stopped loading
Barely living bones
From off the ramp
To stave in slavery
Tortured rules
Experiments on teenaged girls
Slow death
From sudden beatings
Necks half-snapped
Before forced meetings
Standing hours
In mind and snow
Clothed naked
Useless frozen tools
Discarded into ditches whole
Not fat to make a candle from
Life worth less than the paper time
It stopped.

(Try as I might
I see no light
That comes from this
Like Levi
All that's known
Can only make the heart grow dark)

One day
Some sixty years ago

It stopped.

The Christmas Tree - Leszek Engelking

I have lived a solitary life and the management at work, knowing this, send me on business trips at the most inconvenient times of year. Especially one memorable Christmas when the freezing cold, biting wind, and blizzard-like snow made it extremely hard to walk outside. Just think, all those irritating bustling crowds out there, while in here – a whole comfortable compartment for myself!

The train set off on time, but not at its usual speed – snailing forward for hours, slowing down, and then it came to a complete standstill at the third station. No one knew what was going on. Then the loudspeakers announced it would be delayed until further notice. The conductor told us the tracks were covered with thick snow. We wouldn't be moving again for several hours.

I left the train and headed for the station to buy some papers and find a bite to eat. I was thinking of going to a hotel, too, cursing under my breath the weather, state railways, Christmas, my employers, and the whole world.

The Station Café was a ramshackle and run-down place. Even so, I ordered a bowl of flaki and a flat mineral water. I fancied a shot of vodka, but there was none to be had. While eating I heard a strange glassy noise and, turning around, observed a bulky male figure swaying and clambering through the doorway. He was carrying a fully-decorated Christmas tree. Behind him trailed a chord with a plug.

He glared drunkenly in my direction and veered dangerously close to my table before regaining his balance. "The missus kicked me out," he announced with a tone of self-pity. "Said I'd been boozing. So what if I had? Christmas Eve, isn't it? Correct me if I'm wrong?"

Smiling, he glanced at the tree and continued: "I bought it, decorated it, and took it with me. Why should I leave it for that hag?" He gave the tree an appraising look and then blinked with pride and contentment. "Cute tree, ha?"

"Yep, nice to look at" I agreed.

He plunked himself down heavily in the chair opposite me and leaned the tree on the edge of the table. "And you, what, traveling somewhere?"

I nodded.

"Not going anywhere today- that's for sure," he sighed. "All trains are at a standstill. Hopeless situation. No spending Christmas Eve at home tonight. Not a chance. Married?"

"No," I murmured.

"Well, perhaps you're better off for that," he said. "Let's get out of here," he suddenly suggested. "No point in sitting here." He stood up and stumped the tree on the ground like some character in a Christmas play calling for attention.

'Why not?' I thought. 'Nothing better to do.'

At the information desk in the station a bored and irritated woman told me she knew nothing and that I should count myself lucky as many trains were stuck in the middle of the countryside. I got receipt for my baggage and left the station.

The man with the tree marched ahead of me, preoccupied with his role as guide. Taking the public footbridge we came to a street with no traffic. It was getting dark and many of the street lights were on, as well as brightly lit advertisements above the shops, cafés, and restaurants. Snowflakes swirling in the light took on the dazzling colors of a huge Christmas tree. There was hardly anyone around, even though the shops were still open.

I thought the man would lead me straight to the nearest bar, but he just ambled on. We crossed a vast market place and then turned into a steep street. After a few meters my guide shoved open the door to a place that struck me as the worst kind of brawl bar. We were instantly enveloped in a warm fog of beer.

The locals seemed to know him fairly well as they greeted him from behind their tables. Their remarks didn't strike me as all that funny or congenial.

"You're late," laughed one of them. "No one's going exchange your tree for a bottle of vodka at this hour, mate." "What square did you pinch that from, cobba?" asked another. "Take the deco's off the tree and put 'em on, Sunshine! You might pick up some chick!"

I ordered two shots of vodka and some eggs and herring to go with the vodka. "Remember," said the man behind the counter. "We close early today, within the hour."

When my guide had skulled his big shot of vodka, his face brightened with joy. Then he tucked into his herring; he'd obviously developed a taste for it. I ordered a second round and we drank some more. The monotonous drone of the surrounding conversations was slowly sending me into a state of blissful half sleep and I started imagining fields with coppices.

After an hour or so, we left, much to the delight of the proprietor and staff. We found ourselves swaying in the dark street, but we managed to stay on our feet. It was still snowing hard.

"I must find a place to sleep," I said. "Do you know if there's a hotel nearby? I thought I saw one near the Station." The man swayed a bit and waved his hand for me to follow him. Since we were retracing our steps, I didn't question him. The sound of Christmas carols emerged from the snug family homes along the way.

After trudging through the thick snow for some time, I asked, "Where are we going?"

"There's a hall behind the bus station. I used to work in there. Nothing now. Just an empty place but warm, 'cos there are pipes with hot water that go along the walls. I sometimes sleep in there when my old hag drives me mad. There are some blankets and..."

I hesitated for a moment. "Come on! I've got some booze in there. Left for rainy days," he urged. Not very convincing, but on the other hand, I didn't want to be lost in an unknown town.

Soon the dull, red brick hall appeared in front of us. My guide opened a little side door and we entered. My eyes had almost adapted to the dark when I was momentarily blinded by colorful lights of the Christmas tree. He'd placed it on a huge box and just plugged it in. He leaned over and searched for something among a pile of empty boxes.

"There it is!" he cried happily, holding the bottle above his head in a gesture of triumph. "Ain't any glasses here; it goes down better straight from the bottle anyway." I took a cautious sip from the bottle scanning it in vain for a label. It tasted like typical moonshine.

"Why be so modest?" asked my companion as he took a bold quaff, his eyes glittering in the weak light of the tree. Those tiny lanterns were not strong

111

enough to light such a vast space. I found myself depending on my hearing to penetrate the dark, but there were only the approving sighs and grunts of my companion to interrupt the silence. Closing my eyes, I enjoyed the dance of colorful spots under my lids.

Then I heard a squeaking sound and turned toward a little doorway. There I made out two silhouettes in the carnival—two gypsy women in brightly colored dresses studded with sequins and little mirrors.

"Dah, it's so cold outside," said the older one. "Mind if we crash down in here for a while?" The younger one, who may not have even been eighteen, just smiled gently, saying nothing.

My companion said nothing, merely waving the bottle and passing it to the older woman. She took a healthy swig and gave the bottle to the younger one. The girl took a sip and sat near me. I took a swig too and forgot about the label.

"So you sit here all alone?" asked the older one. Then she gave a promising smile to my companion and encouraged him to follow her into the dark. My guide was quite plastered by this time but he got up and they both disappeared from sight. For a moment I heard their giggling, but then all went quiet.

I put my arm around the girl and cuddled her. She did not protest. I explored her fine arms and slim but shapely tail and touched her thick, soft hair. We lay on the Styrofoam 'bed' and it seemed that the time reeled around and rejuvenated us. The Christmas tree was still there but now it looked like a bird about to take flight.

I've no idea why I whispered a word I did not know: "Yggdrasil!"

"How do you know my name?" she asked.

Somewhere in the distance, or maybe in my veins, a train went past. Time was vibrating brightly like fire.

When I woke up in the morning, I was alone. The tree had vanished. My clothes were all right where I'd left them, and my wallet, happily, was there too. Without checking to see if anyone else was in the hall, I gathered up my things and left. Outside it was warmer now. The snow on the pavement was melting under a bright sun.

I easily found the railway station again. Inquiring at the information desk I learned my train had left some time ago but that another would arrive in a few minutes – the only one to run on Christmas day. Good timing for a change, I thought. I ducked into the toilet to freshen up then collected my suitcase and headed for my platform. I meant to buy something to eat but all the cafes and shops were closed. Nobody was waiting for the train. Just then it was announced. It was on time.

The carriages were almost empty. I sat comfortably in a lonely compartment and looked through the window. I saw the hall where I had stayed last night. I saw a star at its roof. "A reminder of communism", I thought, "And fancy that, nobody's thought to remove it!"

Translated by Stefan Bodlewski

Wigilia - Lisa L. Siedlarz

How I love to pretend we are happy.
Christmas Eve, thickening sky, we look

for Gwiazdka, Little Star of Bethlehem,
to begin our feast. At the table we break

oplatek, bread of love, exchange wishes
for happiness and health, bygones forgiven

with a kiss. Hope burns. Like a close family,
we smile over pickled herring, pass beet soup,

red as hell. Warmth a guise for one night where
we get along. Maybe. We do love pretending

on Christmas Eve. Five types of pierogi, flounder,
baked cod. We eat, spirits high. A fairy tale.

The captured Christmas tree wears hundreds of white
lights, a starry sky. Carols complete hearth.

We raise our glasses, na zdrowie, toasting to health.
For years, I've ignored cursing and fights. My feast

has to be perfect. But I've no forgiveness for a brother
who kicked my dog. Twice. In the stomach.

A stepmother who stands beside her son. Now I
understand why my youngest brother just stayed away.

It's time to stop overlooking truth, obvious as night sky.
I can't heal years, the absence of love.

A Christmas Tale - James G. Coon

Marshall Foster watched a solitary tram, nearly empty, soldier up the lonely expanse of ulica Marszałkowska towards the distant promise of a home-cooked meal. Yet no matter how hard he squinted into the crystalline dusk, he could see no such promise for himself, only the certainty of another Christmas Eve spent hungry and alone in Warsaw.

With the tram slowly disappearing into the unseen world somewhere beyond the Palace of Culture and Science, Marshall plodded northward to the intersection of Aleje Jerozolimskie, hoping without expecting to find the coffee shop near the corner still open. Standing there in the cold, the finely grained snow slowly accumulating on his hat and overcoat, he scowled at the shuttered entrance.

In years gone by, the old Forum Hotel would have been a possible substitute, but after refurbishment, it was overpriced, like nearly everything in Centrum, even the now upscale Polonia Hotel, formerly a dive of penultimate resort and home to a once raucous strip club, since closed. He bowed his head in resignation and muttered a cynical remark about the city's freshly minted post-accession sophistication and glamour.

Refusing to admit complete defeat, yet knowing full well he was only delaying the inevitable, Marshall spent the next hour circling several adjacent blocks searching in vain for anything that might be open. By the time he finished his walkabout, the streets were almost deserted. He paused near the steps to the underground, gathering the strength to seek lower company, or at least a stale morsel of something no one else wanted. After taking a deep breath, he gently teetered down the slushy steps.

In short order, Marshall arrived at Au-Bon-Brzuch, the only place before reaching the train station that was always open. In recompense for this convenience, it offered a stomach churning array of gustatory delights, most prominently including stale baguettes garnished with ketchup and cheese whiz. On holidays, the workers added an extra dollop of sarcasm and a sprinkling of churlishness to this savory fare, but after all it was the thought that counted.

Not wanting to walk all the way to the train station, which he typically reserved for a similar problem at Easter, Marshall bellied up to the counter with the resolute intention of making a leisurely selection.

"Whaddyawant?" asked the sour-faced girl behind the counter. She was not much, but Marshall could not forestall the onrush of his decades old fantasy of a ready-to-go romance, even if it came wrapped in such an unlikely package.

"I'm looking," he said, hoping for a smile or a kind word.

"Well, make up your mind," she said, turning to flirt with a couple of dull-eyed rent-a-cops who had sidled up to the stand just beyond the limit of Marshall's peripheral vision.

Marshall was tempted to walk away in silence, but he held his ground, staring longingly yet with a faint disgust at the meagre offering behind the counter. In the end, he chose what he hoped would be the least of all available evils and walked a few paces before stopping to bite into the cardboard-like baguette. As he struggled to force down his Christmas dinner, Marshall's attention fell on a female figure striding purposefully towards the slushy stairs. There was something very familiar about her, but he could not pinpoint what it was without a closer look, so he swallowed hard and trotted after her, trying not to drop the remains of his precious baguette.

He came to an abrupt halt at the bottom of the stairs and looked up. Crouched near the top, with one foot on each of two steps and her body still aimed up the stairs, she had turned her torso and head halfway to face the spot where Marshall stood. The large hood on her hunter green overcoat hid her face in a shadow, but the small diamond-shaped glint of light escaping from the corner of her eye signaled Marshall to follow.

He slowly ascended, as if approaching a deer in the forest, hoping not to scare her off before seeing her face. Slipping on one of the icy steps, he threw the half-eaten baguette into the air and reached for the ground, hoping to break his fall. He slid down several steps before gaining traction. Despite the clamor, she did not move a muscle. He crawled back up a few steps, but just as he was closing in, she flew up the stairs and disappeared in a blur. Marshall scrambled upwards as fast as he could, but when he surfaced, the streets were empty in all directions.

Now the snow fell in little icy chunks that made a gentle tap-tap sound on his rigid woolen hat. Marshall headed home where some tea bags were waiting for him, left over from the previous tenant. Reaching ulica Hoża, he turned left, sighing as he walked in front of his usual kebab place, now closed. A few paces on, he looked to his left at the row of shops behind the paid parking lot. In the morning the usual cadre of drunks would be propped up against the brick wall, arguing over who was entitled to the final soupçon of Christmas vodka left over from the previous evening's devotional services. Even in the winter, with all the windows in his fourth-floor apartment closed, he was sometimes awoken by the sounds of their retching and heaving.

Looking more closely, he saw the hooded mystery lady leaning against the plate glass front of the poster gallery, the left side of her head resting against the glass. Marshall backtracked slightly and padded his way toward the shops, approaching the motionless woman from behind. When he was only two steps away, her right arm shot out to her side. He staggered to a halt, gaping at the long-stemmed white rose in her extended hand. She wiggled the flower, encouraging him to take it. He accepted the flower and found a note wrapped around the stem. Opening the note, he read, "A gift for the disillusioned man."

When he looked up, she had already disappeared. Fearing that the local flatheads might be setting him up for a mugging, he powered the remaining hundred meters to his building and buzzed himself through the door.

A feeling of safety came over Marshall as the door clacked shut behind him. He punched the light switch and forged through the swinging double doors and across the compact entryway to the elevator. The button was already lit. While waiting for it to go off so he could issue his own summons, his mind ran down a well-worn laundry list of regrets and missed opportunities. Over the years it seemed that for each item removed, at least one more surfaced to take its place.

The elevator door abruptly flew open and he found himself face to face with yet another regret—the pleasant-faced lady from upstairs who always smiled at him when their paths crossed. He had often felt tempted to strike up a conversation with her, but thinking it would be just another disappointing waste of time, he had never tried.

"Hi," she said, smiling. "Merry Chris...."

Before she could get the words out, Pani Narzekawska, the old commie baba who lived in the apartment directly beneath Marshall's, barged between them and headed for the swinging doors, her sad-faced husband plodding in her wake.

"Always someone lallygagging in the klatka," she grumbled, bolting through the swinging doors, which immediately swung backwards and knocked her husband to the floor, where he sat with a slightly dazed look on his face. Marshall and the lady from upstairs quickly helped him to his feet. He muttered an embarrassed "thank you" and paddled after his wife, wiping his hands on the sides of his trousers. A few seconds later, upon hearing Pani Narzekawska's piercing voice cursing her husband for not keeping pace, they both exploded with laughter.

"Let me try again. Merry Christmas," she said, extending her hand. "My name is Magda."

"Merry Christmas" he said, handing her the white rose. "My name is Marshall."

"Oh, thank you! How nice!" she said, taking the rose. After a brief and slightly uncomfortable silence, she added, "What a pair those two are! But at least they are entertaining."

"Indeed," Marshall observed in a comically ironic tone. "The building would not be the same without them." The both burst out laughing again.

"Well, I must be going now," she said. "Me too," Marshall replied.

Marshall waited for Magda to exit the building before he flung open the elevator's door and leaped inside. As the door clanged shut, the entryway lights timed out and all was dark. As usual, the bulb in the elevator was broken, but today, instead of cursing under his breath, he fondly recalled an old Polish lesson featuring the sentence, "Tamta żar wka jest do dupy." Yes, he thought, for now, the light bulb is indeed broken, or words roughly to that effect. With a jaunty flourish he pushed number four, propelling the elevator upwards toward the heavenly firmament.

In his apartment, Marshall located the old tea bags, started heating some water, and went to his balcony to watch the snow fall. Looking down, he could see the spot where the hooded mystery woman had given him the white rose. For a moment, he worried that perhaps it had only taken place in his imagination. Then again, he knew that Magda was real. She had been living upstairs for several years. And the rose was real. She said it was. Feeling buoyed by a surge of optimism about the future, he returned to the kitchen to make his tea.

Outside, a golden-haired figure in a hunter-green overcoat skipped east along ulica Hoża, gaily tossing red rose petals into the air.

Notes on Contributors

John a'Beckett (b. Melbourne, Australia, 1948) is a poet and radio playwright. He came to Poland in 1995 on a Potter Foundation Grant for The Melbourne Writers Theatre. A co-founder of New Europe Writers, John is the author of *The Polish Year* and is preparing the chapbook *The High Country*.

Mohamed Ben Younes (b. Thenia, Algeria, 1972) has been living and working in Warsaw since 2004. A poet, novelist, and teacher of French, he won the Best Poem of The Year Award in 2003 for A Country I Love. He recently published his latest novel, Limbo (Seuil).

Anne Berkeley (b. Ludlow, U.K) is part of the poetry group Joy of Six. Her pamphlet "The Buoyancy Aid and other poems" was published by Flarestack in 1997. She won the TLS prize in 2000 and was a prizewinner in the Arvon competition in 2004. Her first full collection, The Men from Praga, was published by Salt in April 2009.

A. Bo (b. Dreamtime, Ukraine) recently surfaced on Closed Circuit TV, Medieval Flash, and No Tube. His scratchings can be peeled off unpublished Bach and have been influenced by James Joyce, Relative Caravanning, and Absolute Vodka.

Ben Borek (b. Camberwell, UK, 1980) is the author of *Donjong Heights*, a 152-page poem about a South London tower block. In 2004, he graduated with distinction from the University of East Anglia with an MA in Creative Writing. He taught English in Warsaw in 2005 and is currently working on his second novel.

Ernest Bryll (b. Warsaw, 1935) is a poet, journalist, translator, movie critic, and eminent presenter of new Polish poetry. The first volume of his verse *Christmas Eves of the Madman*, was published in 1958. From 1991-1995 he was the Polish Ambassador to the Republic of Ireland.

Wojciech Chmielewski (b. Warsaw, 1969) is a fiction writer and a graduate of history and journalism from Warsaw University. He is the author of *The White Boxer* (2006), which was short-listed for the 2007 VI Józef Mackiewicz Literary Award.

James G. Coon (b. Cincinnati, USA, 1950) is a co-founder of New Europe Writers. His work has appeared in *Prague Tales*, *Budapest Tales*, and elsewhere. Currently a resident of Bangkok, he is a frequent visitor to that wondrous land located between the pit of man's fears and the summit of his knowledge. He is working on a follow-up novel to *The Great Gatsby*, set in the less prosperous decade of the 70s.

Jacek Dehnel (b. Gdańsk, 1980) has emerged rapidly to prominence as a poet, and is a graduate of Polish studies at Warsaw University. Widely published, he is the author of *Balzaciana* and has translated Philip Larkin into Polish.

Leszek Engelking (b. Bytom, Poland,1955) is a poet, short-story writer, critic, essayist, scholar, and prolific translator of contemporary Czech literature into Polish. He lives near Warsaw and collaborates with Polish Radio.

Judith Eydmann (b. Surrey, England, 1976) read biological sciences at King's College before pursuing a career in publishing. She writes partly to record all the varieties of the journeys she makes. Her work has featured in various magazines and anthologies.

Andrew Fincham (b. Staffordshire, England, 1964) is a co-founder of New Europe Writers. His poetry has appeared in over a dozen anthologies. The bilingual *Centre of Gravity* (Ibis 2004) received the UNESCO / Poezja Dzisiaj award for foreign poetry in Poland.

Stefan Golston (b. 1904, Warsaw. d. 2006) led an extraordinary yet harrowing life that included an escape from the Nazis stretching from Warsaw to Kaunas, Vladivostok, and Japan. He finally settled in Seattle. Connected with the Telos Writers Group, Stefan translated *The Ghetto Poems* and the poetry of Marian Hemar.

Paula Gutowska (b. Warsaw, 1986) is a student of Law and Fine Arts and laureate of several literary competitions, including O Pióro Prezydenta Warszawy for her poem *Pterodactylus over my Warsaw*.

Jan Himilsbach (b. 1931, Warsaw; d. 1988) was "a grace to our literature," according to Tadeusz Konwicki. Renowned as a self-taught "natural" writer of many short stories, a poet, and by profession, a stonemason. He is also fondly remembered as an actor, especially for his characteristic face and famously hoarse voice and his role in the film *The Cruise*. His *Selected Short Stories* are still popular in Poland.

Hatif Janabi (b. Ghammas, Iraq, 1952) escaped a climate in Iraq highly unfavorable to poetic expression and crossed Turkey, Bulgaria, and Romania to reach Poland in 1976. His most notable volume of poetry is *Questions and Their Retinue.* Describing himself as a tormented traveler, he lives outside Warsaw with his wife and son.

Maria Jastrzębska (b. Warsaw, 1953) grew up the UK and currently lives in Brighton. She is the author of *Postcards from Poland and other correspondences* (Working Press, 1991), as well as being widely published in magazines and anthologies.

Jarosław Klejnocki (b.1963, Warsaw) is a prose writer, poet, essayist, and literary critic. He teaches in a Warsaw secondary school, lectures at Warsaw University, and has co-authored manuals for Polish High Schools.

Marek Kochan (b. Warsaw, 1969) is a novelist, dramatist, and lecturer at Warsaw University. He was written two novels as well as stories and television screenplays. His prose has been translated into Hungarian, Croatian, German, Italian, and Hebrew.

Karen Kovacik (b.Michigan, U.S.A.) is an Associate Professor of English and Director of Creative Writing at Indiana University-Purdue University of Indianapolis. She has published a new collection of poems, in part based on her experience of Warsaw, called *Metropolis Burning.* She visits Poland frequently and is currently translating the poetry of Katarzyna Boruń-Jagodzinska.

Ewa Kowalczyk (b. Żyrardów, Poland, 1985) studied history and sociology at Cardinal Wyszyński University. In 2008 she published her first book of poetry: *Scuse going through.* She belongs to The Zyrardovian Evenings of Poetry.

Paweł Kubiak (b. 1950 Karszew, Poland) studied theology. His first poems were published in 'Zarzewie' in 1973. A member of ZLT, literary critic and editor, he is working on a selection of Vietnamese verse in Polish. His fifth collection is 'Miniatures and Fragments about Love' (2009).

Wojciech Maslarz (b. Kutno, Poland, 1962) is a philologist, English teacher, poet, and translator. He has recently published a chapbook of verse entitled *The Image of the Minotaur* and is Polish Editor of New Europe Writers.

Jacek Podsiadło (b. Szewna, Poland, 1964) is a poet and a prose writer. He has been associated with the BruLion Polish Poetry Group since 1991 and has won many prizes and literary competitions, including the Georg Trakl award in 1994 and Koscielski Prize in 1998. He has written a column for *The General Weekly* since 2000.

Ella Risbridger (b.1992, London) made several trips to Warsaw between the millennium and the accession to Europe. She explores life through assembling words on hand-made paper or on line. Currently living three thousand miles from Poland, she was shortlisted for the UAE Scriptwriter Award 2009.

Jennifer Robertson (b. The Orkneys, U.K.) has lived in Edinburgh, St Peters-burg, Warsaw, and Barcelona. She is the author of 25 books, including poetry (*Ghetto, Loss and Language*) and prose (*Don't Go to Uncle's Wedding- Voices of the Warsaw*). Her latest collection of poems is an e-book, *Clarissa, or Arrested Innocence*.

Stephen Romer (b. Hertfordshire, U.K.,1957) is a poet and lecturer at the University of Tours in France. His latest collection of poetry is *Yellow Studio* (2008), shortlisted for the 2008 T. S. Eliot Prize. He spent time in Poland in the late 1980s teaching English literature at the University of Lodz. This visit in-spired him to write a series of poems that have gained significant popularity.

Carole Satyamurti (b. UK, 1939) lived in America, Singapore, and Uganda before settling in London, where she teaches at the University of East London. She won the first prize in the National Poetry Competition in 1986 and has published two collections with OUP, *Broken Moon* (1987) and *Changing the Subject* (1990)

Lisa L. Siedlarz (b. 1964, New Haven,Connecticut, USA) is a poet whose grand-parents emigrated from Poland in 1911. She has an MFA from WCSU, and is Editor of Connecticut River Review. Publications include: The MacGuffin, Calyx, War, Literature & the Arts, and others. Her debut chapbook, '*I Dream My Brother Plays Baseball*', is from Clemson University Press (2009).

Sławomir Shuty (b. Poland, 1973) is an avowed lover of the Nowa Huty Smelt-ing Works near Krakow, a short story writer, photographer, and director. Best known for *The Screen, The Lamp*, and *God's Spark*. He is the laureate of *The Passport of the Policy*, which won The Cracow Venue Prize in 2004.

John Surowiecki (b. Meriden, Connecticut, 1943) An M.A. in English from the University of Connecticut. he twice won the annual Wallace Stevens Poetry Prize. Now a freelance writer, his work has appeared in many journals and two chapbooks: *Caliban Poems* and *Five-hundred Widowers in a Field of Chamomile.*

Wiktor Sybilski (b. Warsaw, 1978) is an art historian specializing in Russian culture and a translator of German literature. Educated in Warsaw, Munich and London he now lives in Grochow

Joanna Szczepkowska (b. Warsaw, 1953) is an actress, columnist, author, and poet. A 1975 graduate of the Warsaw State Theatre School, she made her debut in the Television Theatre production of Chekhov's *The Three Sisters*. She became known for the announcement: "Ladies and Gentlemen, on the 4th of June, 1989, communism ended in Poland." This is the subject of her latest book.

Grażyna Tatarska (b. Warsaw, 1947) has won several awards for poetry and prose, including in the *Wandering Through My Warsaw* Municipal Literary Competition. She lives in and writes about the Warsaw district of Praga.

Leo Yankevich (b. USA, 1961) is a leading poet of The New Formalist movement whose poems and translations have appeared in over 100 journals on both sides of the Atlantic, including *Chronicles*, *The London Magazine*, *London Poetry Review*, and *The Pennsylvania Review*. He came to Poland in the Eighties and now lives in Gliwice in Upper Silesia.

Notes on Translators

Stefan Bodlewski (b. Warsaw, 1971) studied English Philology at the University of Lodz.. He has translated the poetry of Kenneth Slessor and admits to a weakness for black jelly beans and vintage car rallies.

Jennifer Croft (b. Oklahoma, U.S.A.) holds an MFA in Translation and is currently completing her PhD in Comparative Literature at Northwestern University. She has translated work by Olga Tokarczuk, Hanna Krall, and Marzanna Kielar. She lives in Paris.

Karolina Maślarz (b. Warsaw, 1984) graduated from Warsaw University, Institute of English Studies with an M.A. in translation. She has participated in a Socrates-Erasmus student exchange at Charles University (Prague) and has translated Polish authors like Slavomir Mrożek and Marek Nowakowski.

Wojciech A. Maślarz (b. Kutno, Poland, 1962), Polish Editor of New Europe Writers, is a translator as well as contributor to Warsaw Tales.

Katarzyna Waldegrave (b. London, 1942) was raised in New Zealand and resides in Wellington. She is a translator of Mrożek and other writers and teaches English and Social Science.